LAUREN YANOFSKY HATES THE HOLOCAUST

LAUREN YANOFSKY HATES THE HOLOCAUST

Leanne Lieberman

ORCA BOOK PUBLISHERS

Library and Archives Canada Cataloguing in Publication

Lieberman, Leanne, 1974-
Lauren Yanofsky hates the Holocaust / Leanne Lieberman.

Issued also in electronic formats.
ISBN 978-1-4598-0109-7

I. Title.
PS8623.I36L39 2013   jc813'.6   C2012-907465-9

First published in the United States, 2013
Library of Congress Control Number: 2012952950

Summary: Lauren, a Jewish teen, is sick of hearing about the Holocaust
but must make a tough choice when some friends play Nazi war games.

*Orca Book Publishers is dedicated to preserving the environment and has printed this book on
Forest Stewardship Council® certified paper.*

Orca Book Publishers gratefully acknowledges the support for its publishing
programs provided by the following agencies: the Government of Canada through
the Canada Book Fund and the Canada Council for the Arts, and the Province of British
Columbia through the BC Arts Council and the Book Publishing Tax Credit.

ONTARIO ARTS COUNCIL
CONSEIL DES ARTS DE L'ONTARIO

Design by Teresa Bubela
Cover photography by Gary McKinstry
·Author photo by Bernard Clark

ORCA BOOK PUBLISHERS   ORCA BOOK PUBLISHERS
PO Box 5626, Stn. B   PO Box 468
Victoria, BC Canada   CUSTER, WA USA
V8R 6S4   98240-0468

www.orcabook.com
Printed and bound in Canada.

16   15   14   13   •   4   3   2   1

For Robbie Stocki

One

On the first morning of grade eleven, my mom is waiting for me in our kitchen. She's made me a plate of eggs and toast and tucked an envelope under my glass of orange juice. She glances at my ripped jeans but doesn't say anything about them. Her shiny white suit seems a little over-the-top for her nutritionist job at the hospital, but then Mom is often overdressed.

I sit down at the table and hold up the envelope. "What's this?"

Mom slides her gold-streaked hair behind her ear and keeps making my brother Zach's lunch. "Just open it."

I sip my juice and frown at the return address. It's my parents' temple, which means it's from either the Jewish youth group or the Hebrew school. I chuck it aside and dig into my eggs and toast.

Mom is very involved at the temple. Her latest project is a mitzvah, or "good deed," committee that brings food to elderly people or baby presents to new moms.

Mom ignores the fact that I've tossed the envelope aside. "So, first day of school," she says.

"Yep."

"Excited?"

"No." I am a little bit, but I wouldn't admit that to her.

Mom says, "The temple's after-school program also starts today."

"I'm aware of that." I squint at the envelope.

"Your father and I are hoping you'll go this year."

"Not a chance." I shovel eggs into my mouth.

Mom sighs. "It's only two nights a week."

I glare at her. "I'm not going. Ever."

"Don't you want to get your driver's license?"

Because I've refused to do any Jewish activities lately, I haven't been allowed to get my license. "It's better for the environment to walk or bike," I mutter.

Mom shuts the refrigerator a little more forcefully than necessary. "It's not like we're asking a lot."

I stand up and wrap my remaining toast in a paper towel and shove my dishes into the dishwasher. "When are you going to give this up?"

"Lauren..." Mom says, but I've already grabbed my lunch from the fridge, picked up my bag and am headed to the front door.

It's a beautiful, crisp morning, sunny with a light breeze. I take a moment to clear my head and put on some lip gloss. Then I head down the street toward school.

I love my walk to school. All the years I went to Jewish day school, I was confined to a car pool, squished in the backseat of either my mom's wagon or Shayna Shuster's van, which always reeked of her perfume. Now that I go to regular high school, it no longer matters to me what time Mom manages to pry Zach out of bed; I leave on my own time.

First I walk down my street, with the maples rustling overhead. Then I cut through the park, the dew collecting on my flats. The mountains are a deep blue against the lighter blue of the sky. On the other side of the park, a few blocks away, is my school.

I am lucky because not only do I have a great walk but also a pretty good school. There are no metal detectors or drug busts or gangs, just regular kids coming to school.

Okay, so most kids don't take the time to appreciate their school—it does sound pretty pathetic—but on the first day, I'm always thankful, because I wasn't supposed to go to public high school. I was supposed to attend (cue the music from *Jaws*) The Akiva Jewish High School. My parents wanted me to spend five more years with the same cliquey, mean kids I'd endured since kindergarten.

But I put my foot down. I pulled out all the stops, including my trump card: I told my mother I'd stop eating if I had to go to Hebrew high school. This was very effective because Mom works with anorexic girls. I even went on a two-day hunger strike, although I cheated and ate a steady supply of licorice and Ritz crackers when no one was looking.

Here are the six reasons I gave my parents for letting me go to public school:

1. Public school has a better basketball team.
2. Public school kids are nicer, especially my friends Brooke, Chloe and Em.
3. The whole world is not Jewish, and no one should pretend it is by going to a school that is all Jewish.
4. Akiva was sure to be social purgatory for me. Did my parents want me to need many, many years of expensive therapy?
5. Public school is free. My parents could save the tuition and take our family to Hawaii instead.
6. Public school has better language programs. What if I wanted to take Mandarin or Cantonese? The Jewish school doesn't offer these, and if I want to go into business, another language would be a huge asset.

Okay, so number six is a little weak. I've had three years to learn a new language and I've stuck with French. Also, I have no intention of going into business.

When I get to school, I make my way to D wing, where my friends and I always have our lockers, near the cute boys from our class.

Brooke is already shoving her bag and running shoes into her locker and attaching a magnetic mirror to the locker door. She tightens her blond ponytail and waves at me when she sees me coming down the hall. Brooke has been my best friend since we met on a soccer team when we were ten. Now we play on the basketball team together, and since we're in grade eleven this year, we'll both be starters. Most of the time I can beat Brooke when we play one-on-one, even though she's a couple of inches taller than me. I can be surprisingly fast, and I have longer arms.

"What's your first class?" Brooke asks. We compare timetables and give each other a high five when we realize we both have biology first period and phys ed after lunch.

The first bell rings, and after checking to make sure my hair hasn't frizzed, Brooke and I head up the stairs to class. We choose seats in the middle of the room, not too close to the front, or we'll look like geeks, but not so far back that we'll be tempted to whisper to each other and get in trouble.

Brooke and I are talking with Mac Thompson and Tyler Muller, two guys who have lockers in our wing, when Brooke grips my hand under the lab table. She's staring at the doorway, where Jesse Summers stands, scanning the room for a place to sit. There are still plenty of empty seats, but he looks right at me, smiles and then heads toward us. I think Brooke might faint. I have to shake her hand off mine so Jesse doesn't see us holding hands and think we're weird.

Jesse slides onto the stool next to me and says, "Hi, Lauren."

"Hi."

"How was your summer?"

"Good. You?"

"Good, really good."

Before my stomach actually catapults my breakfast out of my mouth, the biology teacher, Mr. Saunders, starts handing out textbooks and course outlines.

I'm trying to focus on Mr. Saunders, but sitting beside me is the cutest guy in our school. No, possibly in the universe. Jesse is tall and lean with dark skin and hair. He also has the most beautiful cheekbones, what Brooke calls "radiant facial structure." Personally, I'm more interested in the way his jeans hang off his hips and the way he flips his hair out of his eyes. Brooke and I spent a lot of time last spring walking by his house when he got back from boarding school. "That's where he lives," Brooke would say, and then we'd both sigh. I would rather have been playing soccer or hanging out at Brooke's, but Brooke always wanted to walk by and see if he was around.

Attractive guys we know usually fall into one of two categories: (1) cute, goofy guys we wouldn't date because we've known them for years or (2) cute guys who don't go to our school who we would go out with, if only they'd ask.

Jesse fits into a whole other category: guys who are so gorgeous and so untouchable, we can only stare. And it's not like I'm gorgeous myself. I have clear skin and an olive complexion, and I'm dark enough that sometimes people at my parents' temple ask me if I'm a sabra, which means a native-born Israeli. Other than that, I have ordinary dark eyes and a biggish nose. My most challenging feature is definitely my hair. It's long and dark brown and very curly. I've been begging to get it chemically straightened, but Mom won't let me.

I endure a whole hour of Brooke sitting on one side of me while Jesse lounges on his stool on the other side, foot tapping, pen flipping, totally distracting me. I know she's dying to text me to say *WTF?* or *OMG*.

When class ends, Brooke and I hurry out of the room, our shoulders pressed together. "Omigod," she says, "I can't believe he talked to you."

"I can't believe he sat next to me."

"We'll probably sit like that all term." She elbows me in the side. "Lucky girl."

I'm so nervous all I can do is tug on the ends of my hair.

Brooke and I split up after that because I have English and Brooke is off to math.

When I get to English class, Jesse is sitting by the windows. "Holy fuck," I whisper to myself as I find a seat on the other side of the room, at the back. I take out my phone and text Brooke. U won't believe who's in English.

God? she writes back.

Yes.

It's destiny.

I don't think so.

Then the bell rings, and I put my phone away.

I have Mr. Willoughby for English again, which is great. Some of the guys call him a fag and make fun of the way he uses words like *Augustine* or *imperative* or *disingenuous*. It doesn't matter to me if he's helping us understand Steinbeck by lecturing on the social structure of farm labor or the boll weevils of the dust bowl—I'm riveted. It's not what he says, it's how he says it in his British accent, his long arms waving around his fiery red hair.

But today, not even Mr. Willoughby can distract me from the back of Jesse's perfect head.

By the time I get back to my locker for lunch, Brooke is already there, chatting with our friend Chloe. I can tell from the dreamy expression on Brooke's face that they are talking about Jesse. Chloe is shorter than Brooke and me and curvier, despite being on a perpetual diet. She has blond hair, recently cut to a bob, and green eyes. She dances competitively and has really strict parents. Her dad is so mean, he doesn't even talk to us when we come over.

Chloe puts her arm around my shoulders. "I hear you are the *luckiest* girl ever."

"It's not that big a deal."

"Are you kidding?" Chloe elbows me in the ribs. "He *talked* to you."

"Well, that's 'cause we used to know each other."

Chloe shakes her head. "It's really not fair."

"Guys, get a grip. He said, 'Hi, how are you.'"

"An excellent start," Brooke says. "Now you need to renew the friendship."

I roll my eyes and pull my lunch bag out of my locker.

"I wonder why he's in our grade this year," I say.

"I heard he flunked out of a bunch of stuff at boarding school, then dropped out for a while," Brooke says.

It's weird. I used to know Jesse really well because he lives down the street from me. When I was in grade seven and he was in grade eight, we played a lot of basketball after school. That was the year my closest school friend, Alexis, moved to Seattle, and Rebecca Shuster formed the I-Hate-Lauren clique at my Hebrew day school. I was taller than all the other kids, my hair had erupted into this giant Jew-fro, and I had glasses *and* braces. I spent every recess playing basketball with the boys while the girls snickered. I'd come home after school, friendless and miserable, and play more basketball with Jesse. I was already five foot eight, and Jesse was only five foot three. Now he is taller than me.

When I started high school, we stopped hanging out together. His locker was in another wing of the school, and I felt too shy to talk to him. While I was hanging out with Chloe, Brooke and Em, he was skipping classes and getting expelled for breaking into the school gym to shoot hoops on weekends.

Before anyone can say anything else, Em comes racing down the hallway, dodging guys from the basketball team and Smoker girls. Em is the youngest of five kids, all much older than her, so only one sister still lives at home. Em lives in the biggest house I've ever seen. It has two staircases, but most of it's really shabby. The kitchen hasn't been renovated since at least 1980, and there's real shag carpet in the basement.

Red hair flying, glasses slipping down her nose, she skids on her flats and has to grab Chloe. "You won't believe what the musical is going to be this year."

"Oh, do tell us," Brooke says, sounding totally bored.

Em ignores her and takes Chloe by the shoulders. "It's *Grease!*"

They start hugging each other and jumping all over the hall. "This is amazing," Chloe shouts.

The guys stare at Chloe and Em, and Brooke and I step away.

Our high school puts on a musical every second year. Last time it was *The Pajama Game*, and Chloe and Em were in the chorus because we were only in grade nine. Since there won't be a musical next year, this is their year.

And, oh yeah, they're obsessed with *Grease*. They already know all the songs and choreography from the movie. All through grades eight and nine, on a typical Saturday night we watched either *High School Musical* or *Grease* or reenacted scenes from them. Even I know all the lyrics to "Summer Nights" and I can't carry a tune. Chloe and Em's favorite song is "You're the One That I Want," which they sing at the drop of a hat. It's cute, but also sort of annoying.

I go to the bathroom to distance myself from Chloe and Em, and when I get back, Brooke isn't where I left her. I gaze down the hallway and see her sitting on the floor with Chantal Matthews and some of the other Smoker girls. I don't really know Chantal. It's not that I don't like her or anything; she's just not into basketball or any of the theater stuff that Chloe and Em do. Chantal's always wearing too much makeup and showing too much cleavage. Her long red fingernails make me think of vampires. She usually sits at the back of every class, although I know she's smart at math. I saw her test by accident last year, and she got an almost perfect score, even on the story problems.

I walk back to where Chloe and Em are sitting. "What's up with that?" Chloe says, tilting her head toward Brooke.

We all stare down the hall a moment, and then I sit down and get out my lunch. Chloe and Em start talking about *Grease* again. Chloe wants to know if the boys will get to sing the raunchy lines from the "Greased Lightning" song and if they'll have to smoke onstage. I try to catch Brooke's eye, but she and Chantal get up and start heading down the hall toward the doors leading to the back field. Chantal usually spends her lunch hour with the rest of the Smokers under the big willow at the back of the field. After Brooke and Chantal go out, I slowly make my way down the hall to the double doors. I catch a glimpse of Brooke as she disappears under the long, drooping branches of the tree.

Two

After lunch I have phys ed, followed by history with Mr. Whiteman. I had him last year too, and he's my favorite teacher in the whole school. He doesn't tell a lot of jokes or give you projects like making a comic strip about Quebec nationalism, but the essays and debates he assigns always make you think.

At the end of the day, Chloe and Em are off to a youth-group event at their church. Em has always been religious—she even goes to Bible study in the morning—but I'm pretty sure Chloe only goes to check out the guys.

Since Brooke was late for gym class, I don't have a chance to talk to her until the end of the day, when I corner her by her locker. "What's with eating lunch with the Smokers?"

"Drama talk is for losers." Brooke pulls out her bag.

"Since when are you not a loser?" I tease Brooke, hip-checking her into her locker.

Brooke sticks out her tongue. "This year I'm into change. Wanna go for a run?"

I shrug. "You sure you want to run with a loser?"

"Only because I can cream you."

Brooke and I walk to her house and change into our running clothes. Brooke used to live close to me in an even bigger house than mine, but her parents got divorced this summer. Now she lives in a townhouse near school. Brooke had to help move instead of coming to basketball camp with me for the last three weeks of August.

From Brooke's house we race uphill to my house. It's our standard run, and Brooke usually wins, but I did some research on sprinting and realized I've been starting my sprint too early. Today I let Brooke pull ahead and don't pick up my pace until I'm almost at the top of the hill. I sail past her easily and then cruise down my street. I even slow down so she can see my graceful arrival into my driveway. Brooke sticks out her tongue when she catches up, panting and huffing. She picks up my basketball from where it's resting by the net and starts dribbling fiercely. "I'm going to kill you now."

When I was still in Hebrew-school hell, I would look forward to the weekends when Brooke and I would hang out and spend hours making forts out of cushions and blankets.

When we got sick of the fort, we'd play soccer in her yard or basketball in the driveway.

Sometimes Brooke would come by my house on her bike and we'd go exploring. Before Brooke, I had only biked the streets around my house, a series of curved avenues boxed in by what my brother and I called "the busy streets." Brooke fearlessly crossed major intersections, leading us blocks away from home. When I'd asked her if she was allowed to bike that far away, she shrugged and said, "I dunno. I never asked."

Brooke's life was like that. In my house, play dates were scheduled by my mother in advance, and snacks were carefully and punctually prepared: neatly arranged cut-up fresh fruits and vegetables, homemade banana bread and—my favorite—peanut-butter-and-banana sandwiches on whole-grain bread. In her house, Brooke merely helped herself to processed-cheese squares or granola bars whenever she wanted.

Brooke's bike routes took us farther and farther away from home, and soon we were biking down to the beach, where we would chase seagulls and build elaborate sand castles. It was a gentle downhill ride on the way there, and a long uphill climb home. Brooke, being competitive, liked to race me up the hills, but because I was taller than her then—taller than everyone until grade nine, when the guys started to catch up—I could always beat her.

Brooke introduced me to Chloe and Em at her sleepover birthday party the year we turned eleven. I immediately liked their goofy enthusiasm. While the Hebrew-school kids were obsessing about what brand of jeans they wore and how their hair looked and who had the fanciest bat mitzvah, Brooke, Chloe and Em were putting on plays in Em's basement and taking the bus to go swimming at the Kitsilano pool down by the beach. Instead of going to Jewish camp to be indoctrinated with Zionist propaganda, Brooke, Chloe and Em spent two weeks camping on the Oregon coast in a Volkswagen Westfalia with Em's parents. They got to make campfires and roast marshmallows. I had to sing Zionist songs and play war games where we pretended to battle Arabs.

I dubbed my three friends The Perfects. Everything about them—their hair and their cute clothes, the way they always had so much fun—seemed bright and shiny. I wanted to be just like them, and I wanted to go to high school with them.

Brooke and I play basketball for half an hour, sweating in the warm afternoon sun and laughing at each other's missed shots. Then Mom pulls into the driveway in her station wagon. She barely even looks at us before going into the house.

"What's up with her?" Brooke says.

"She's mad at me again." I bounce the ball hard against the pavement.

"Gee, what did you do, touch the walls?"

I flash a grin at her. The first time Brooke came to our house, Mom asked her not to touch the walls because she might leave fingerprints. Brooke refers to my house as "the museum." Unlike most of the other houses in my neighborhood, our house is really modern. From the street it looks like a giant glass box, except you can't see into it because of all the trees and frosted glass. The whole back of the house is glass too. Inside, our house is very white. The kitchen is white, the living room is white, and, well, everything is white and made out of shiny materials I can't identify. The living room isn't for sitting in, more for looking at. I rarely have friends over because there's nowhere to hang out except the family room, and Mom's always there, getting in the way.

Mom tried to decorate my room in all white too, so the house would be "consistent," but I insisted on painting my desk blue and having a blue bedspread and blue blinds. My room feels like the ocean while the rest of the house is the sky on a hot day.

"It's too complicated to get into," I say and focus on trying to sink another basket. Then I sit down on the steps to stretch my legs. Brooke joins me. "I'll pick up my bag in the morning on the way to school," I say.

"I could drop it off tonight, if you like."

"Nah, that's okay. I don't need anything in it until tomorrow."

Brooke grins. "I might be going out tonight anyway, on a mission. Want to come?"

"What kind of mission?"

"Oh, just a visit to my dad's."

Brooke's dad left her mom and lives with another woman a few blocks away. But it's no secret Brooke's parents had the worst marriage ever—they barely talked to each other—and both of them seem much happier now that they're apart.

"To do what?" I bunch my fists on my legs. Recently Brooke told me that she and her sister put water in her dad's fuel tank to mess up his car.

"I haven't decided yet," Brooke says.

I'm spared having to answer by Mom sticking her head out the side door. "Could you please come in and help out now?" She licks her lips the way she does when she's pissed off.

Brooke and I say goodbye, and I go in to set the table for dinner. Mom focuses on making pasta sauce, dicing up mushrooms and peppers. My dad cuts up vegetables for a salad, humming along to a jazz station on the radio in his tuneless way. I avoid looking at Mom and take a quick survey of the kitchen for the envelope I didn't open earlier. I don't see it, but stuck under a refrigerator magnet is the announcement for Hebrew school. When Mom isn't looking, I quietly crumple it up and shove it into the recycling bin under the sink.

Dad coughs.

I give him my most innocent look. "What?"

Dad sighs. "So, how was the first day of school?"

"Fine. The usual." I always say this, although today it's not exactly true. I think about Jesse for a moment and then about Brooke ditching me at lunch.

"And how was your first day?" I ask. "Did you instruct the youth of today on Jewish destruction?" Dad teaches an introductory university course on the Holocaust each fall.

Dad swats me with a dishcloth. "Classes don't start until next week."

Even though Dad's a Holocaust historian, he's a pretty cheerful guy. When he's not reading depressing books about the slaughter of European Jews, he obsesses over his golf game and eats deli sandwiches, pickles and pretzels. He also likes basketball, but he can't play anymore because he has lower-back issues and won't do the Pilates exercises his physiotherapist recommended.

When I finish the table, Mom asks me to unload the dishwasher. I don't dare say no. It's the only thing she says to me the whole time.

When dinner is ready, Dad asks me to get Zach.

I find Zach in the front hall, threading red K'Nex pieces through the rails of the banister up to the second floor. "Adding some color?" I say. He ignores me and keeps adding pieces and making airplane noises until I get in his face and tell him we're having pasta. Zach is twelve and kind of bizarre. You can call him for dinner all you like, but if he's engaged in something he'll tune you out. Zach doesn't have interests, he has obsessions. Lately he's been into flight. It started with birds—bird-watching, bird books, hawks, the Audubon Society, endangered wetlands, migration and hawks.

Zach's bird fixation began because Mom got this nutty idea that the eagles living down the street were my grandparents—Dad's parents—reincarnated. She wasn't serious; she just liked the idea. Well, Zach had a hard time with the distinction between Mom greeting the birds as if they were my grandparents and the eagles really *being* my grandparents.

Anyway, Zach is done with birds now and has moved on to flying machines: planes, helicopters, jets, rockets, etc. He started with a grand survey of all flying machines and is now fixated on biplanes. Zach can talk at length about planes like the Fairey Swordfish, a torpedo bomber used during the Second World War. This fall he is supposed to start studying for his bar mitzvah, a celebration that marks the beginning of adulthood for Jewish boys when they're thirteen. You have to read a blessing over the Torah—

a sacred Jewish text—and there's a party afterward. Most kids also lead the service and chant part of the Torah. Girls have a similar celebration, except it's called a bat mitzvah. Zach isn't very keen on having a bar mitzvah, but my parents have promised him a ride in a biplane if he'll go through with it.

After dinner I leave the whiteness of the main floor and head downstairs to the basement, which is unfinished. I guess Mom couldn't imagine an all-white basement too, so it's just for storage. Sometimes Zach and I play floor hockey on the concrete floor, when he's in the mood.

I head to Dad's workbench, where tools are stored next to old paint cans and extra flooring. The workbench is a bit of a joke. Dad can't do anything more complex than change lightbulbs and tighten screws. Mom doesn't even let him paint anymore. Dad likes to hold up his hands and say, "These are the hands of an academic." He thinks this is superfunny.

I'm using the workbench to make a lantern for next summer's lantern festival at Trout Lake Park. Brooke took me to the festival this summer, and I loved it. At first I couldn't imagine what a lantern festival would be like. A bunch of kids with Chinese lanterns hanging out in a park? It sounded lame. Then we got to the park, and I saw people walking around with all kinds of different homemade lanterns. There were cupcake lanterns and animal lanterns and lanterns shaped like the moon.

Brooke had brought a lantern she'd made to look like a basketball. When she put an LED light inside it, the whole thing glowed. It was supercool. I'd wished it had a real candle in it, but Brooke said she couldn't figure out how to keep it from catching fire.

The lantern festival wasn't just about lanterns. There was music too, and people were wearing costumes and doing weird theatrical performances. Women dressed as fairies with big wire-and-net wings gave out handfuls of silver powder to blow for making wishes. A marching band of accordions and drums passed in a cacophony of sound. Brooke and I stopped by the lake to listen to a Chinese percussion band with chimes and gongs and other instruments I couldn't identify. There were stilt-walkers and fireworks and a troupe of women gyrating in hula hoops lit on fire. "Wow, it's like the circus," Brooke said.

"Yeah, but better." I'd stared at the women with the fiery hula hoops and wondered what it would be like to be surrounded by fire and not get burned. Maybe it was like pulling your finger through a candle flame so quickly that you didn't get singed, except you would be pulling your whole body through the flame.

When we were heading out of the park to leave, I saw a group of people picnicking, surrounded by glowing paper-bag lanterns. Sitting away from the crowds, they had marked their area with a circle of light. I stopped and looked and let out a long sigh.

I'd seen candles used a zillion times before, but never like this. Mom was always lighting candles for the different Jewish holidays, marking those special times, but these candles in the park were marking a special space. I'd looked longingly at the paper-bag lanterns, and then one of the picnickers, a young woman, noticed Brooke and me. She beckoned. "Come join us." The woman stood up and carefully moved a few of the lanterns to make the circle bigger. I looked at Brooke and she shrugged, so we sat down on the grass inside the ring of lanterns. The people kept chatting softly, and Brooke and I sat without talking, staring at the glow of the flickering flames. We sat there for a long time, until we had to leave to make our curfew.

So now I've got tissue paper, some light wood, glue and a saw. I even took a lantern-making course with Brooke, but I haven't quite decided what to make.

I stay downstairs until after ten, trying to sketch an idea for a lantern, and then I go to the kitchen to get a snack. The house is quiet, and most of the lights are off. I pour myself a bowl of cereal and sit at the counter in the dim light. Then Dad comes in and turns on the lights under the cabinets. "I thought I heard you in here." He sits down next to me.

"Hungry," I say, eating more cereal.

Dad taps his fingers on the counter and then runs his fingers through his beard the way he does when he's thinking about something. Finally, I say, "Is Mom really mad?"

"I think just frustrated."

I shudder. "I hate it when she's mad at me."

"She just wants you to be involved, to do something in the community."

I make a face. "I'd rather try archery or knitting."

"What about the youth group? You could try that again, couldn't you?"

"Um, I could think about it."

Dad pats my hand. "That would probably make Mom happy to hear."

"I said I could think about it," I say cautiously.

Dad sighs. "That's a good first step." Then he grabs my head before I can protest and kisses me on the forehead. "Don't stay up too late."

I sit for another few minutes in the kitchen and then head upstairs to bed, turning out lights as I go.

I wish I could tell Dad the real reason I won't go to Jewish high school and why I don't want to be involved in the Jewish community. It's the most important reason, but not one I'm ever going to tell my parents.

Reason number seven: I'm not Jewish anymore.

If I had to answer a census, then yes, I, Lauren Yanofsky, come from Jewish heritage, but I stopped being

Jewish three and a half years ago. People who convert to Judaism are called "Jews by choice." Well, I decided to become a "non-Jew by choice." This doesn't mean I've just assimilated and want to be like everyone else. It means I'm really, truly, not a Jew.

And it's all because of the Holocaust.

I decided not to be Jewish the year I was thirteen, shortly after my bat mitzvah. Dad had promised me pro-basketball tickets if I agreed to visit a new Holocaust memorial at the Jewish cemetery with him. So one very damp April afternoon, I reluctantly got into the car with him and Grandma Rose.

Because Dad is a Holocaust historian, I already knew too much about the destruction of European Jewry during the Second World War. I was always being dragged off to see some Holocaust memorial or attend some convention. I'd been to the Holocaust museum in Washington and to Yad Va'shem, a huge Holocaust museum in Israel, and I'd even been on a tour of Polish concentration camps. My mom and Zach and I had done some fun stuff on those trips while Dad was doing research, but only after we'd endured our share of death, destruction, remembering and commemorating. Some kids got Disney. I got Hitler.

On the way to the cemetery, Grandma Rose sat in the front seat and clucked her tongue against her teeth as she and Dad discussed my cousin Molly's bat mitzvah.

I slouched in the backseat, trying to ignore their conversation. Grandma Rose was horrified that there would be no Sunday-morning brunch or Friday-night dinner.

"What about the out-of-town guests?" Grandma Rose said. "You have to entertain." I could see her lip curling.

"I think they want to keep it a small affair," Dad said.

Grandma Rose sniffed. "You mean a cheap affair."

"Well, that may be true," Dad admitted.

Grandma Rose had strong feelings about how things should be and look. My own bat mitzvah, which she'd help my mom plan, had been a multiday, highly coordinated series of dinners and parties with matching flowers, napkins and invitations, all in baby pink, my least favorite colour.

My Jewish friends all called their grandmothers Bubbie, or Bubba, and their grandfathers Zeydi, the Yiddish words for grandmother and grandfather. I couldn't imagine calling Grandma Rose Bubbie. She was too formal, and she never spoke Yiddish. Grandma Rose was tall, with great legs and beautiful white hair that she had styled weekly. She owned a vast collection of raincoats and matching umbrellas. I didn't know Grandma Rose well, even though she lived only ten minutes away by car. She was quiet and liked listening to classical music. She found our house, and my brother and me, too loud. This was weird, because her husband, our zeydi, had been a very loud guy. He had a big tummy and a big voice, and he gave such strong bear hugs, your back cracked. When we were little, he was always pulling nickels out of our ears or tossing us over his shoulder and yelling, "Sack of potatoes for sale!" Zeydi would give us Reese's Peanut Butter Cups and not care if we got the leather seats of his Cadillac sticky. When Zeydi passed away a few years ago from prostate cancer, Grandma Rose became even more quiet and reserved.

When we arrived at the cemetery, it was so damp outside, it felt like the rain was suspended in the air. I unenthusiastically got out of the car and pulled my hood over my hair. Dad offered me a spot under his big golf umbrella, but I held back and let him and Grandma Rose walk ahead. We made our way past the section where Zeydi was buried and over to a stone monument where the rabbi and a bunch of people from my parents' temple were gathered. I wondered how long this would take. Half an hour? More? It started to drizzle, and I wished I'd listened to Mom and worn my boots. I tugged the drawstrings around my hood tighter so that my hair wouldn't frizz and moved under Dad's umbrella.

The rabbi started making a speech about the Holocaust, how we should always remember the six million who had died. I tuned him out. I knew what he was going to say: forgive but never forget. I thought instead about going to Whistler for a last weekend of spring skiing, and how great basketball camp was going to be that summer. I wondered if I'd be able to convince Mom that colored contact lenses were a "need" and not a "want." The rabbi began the Kaddish, the prayer for the dead, and I murmured the words, thinking about which pictures I'd hang in my locker when I finally got to high school. I'd heard the Kaddish a million times, at each of the Holocaust memorials I'd been dragged to and a zillion times at my Jewish day school. Yeah, yeah, yeah, I thought. All people die eventually.

Then the rabbi started reading out a list of the dead people whose names were carved on the stone memorial. I dug my toe into the wet grass and stared at my sneakers. I was wondering how rude it would be to check my phone when I heard the rabbi call out the name Leibowitz, Grandma Rose's maiden name. It's a pretty common Jewish name, but I remembered Grandma Rose having said she was the only one in Vancouver with that name. I let go of my phone, stopped pawing at the grass and looked up at the rabbi. He was reading out more Leibowitz names. Five, six, seven...I pressed my fingers into my palms, counting. I looked up at Dad's face. His eyes were blank, staring straight ahead. His lips had disappeared into his beard the way they did whenever he was angry. Then I looked at Grandma Rose. Her lined face had crumpled like a crushed piece of paper. I stared in amazement. She'd always been so composed, and now she looked like one of those wizened apple dolls. Tears streamed down her cheeks, her mascara flowing like dark rivers into her wrinkles.

When the rabbi began the final prayers, Grandma Rose's quiet tears changed to long wailing sobs, drowning out the rabbi. Dad wrapped his arm around her shoulders. The rabbi finished reciting the prayer, and Grandma Rose kept crying. Then she walked very slowly to the stone monument, dropped to her knees and lay down on the base of the stone. I hung back, stunned. I'd never seen Grandma Rose cry or express any emotion stronger than distaste, and there she was with her legs splayed on the stone, her pumps hanging off her heels. Dad ran and leaned over her, trying to get her up. He was crying too, the tears running down his face. His beard must be getting wet, I thought. Then Dad was down on his knees too, sort of trying to get Grandma Rose up, but rocking back and forth with her. Grandma Rose was stroking the words engraved into the stone: *Lydia Leibowitz*. And below them, *Sol Leibowitz, Yuri Leibowitz*—a whole line of Leibowitzes. I counted eleven names.

I just stood there, staring down at Dad and Grandma on the stone. Grandma was speaking in Yiddish and English. She said, "They killed my Lydia." Lydia was her sister; I was named in her memory. Both of us had the same Hebrew name, Leah. Luckily, my parents decided to call me Lauren. Lydia sounded so old-fashioned.

I'd always thought the Holocaust was a disaster that happened to other people's families. Grandma Rose and Zeydi had each emigrated separately from Russia before the Second World War and then met in Vancouver. Mom's parents were born in Canada. Yet I'd known Grandma Rose came to Canada without the rest of her family. Why hadn't I ever wondered about them? Even though I was named after Lydia, I'd never thought about how she died or how old she was when she died.

I walked back to the car alone and waited for Dad and Grandma Rose. They came a few minutes later, hunched over and holding on to each other. We silently got into the car and Dad pulled out of the parking lot. No one said anything as we drove. We said goodbye to Grandma Rose when we dropped her off at her condo, but that was it.

Back at home, Dad had gone into the kitchen and poured himself a glass of scotch, even though it was only two in the afternoon. Then I'd followed him into his office. He cleared a stack of papers off a hardback chair for me, and I sat across the desk from him. I felt very grown-up, sitting in his office surrounded by his shelves of books and his messy papers.

Dad sipped his scotch, lined up his pencils on his desk and gazed out the window above one of the bookshelves. Finally I said, "I don't understand."

Dad drummed his fingers on the desk. "What part?"

I wanted to say, *I thought it didn't happen to us.* Instead, I said, "I thought Grandma Rose's family survived the war."

He sighed. "A few did."

"And the rest of them?"

Dad rubbed his eyes.

I wanted to say, *The Nazis killed them, right?* but it sounded too harsh. So I asked, "What happened?"

Dad looked over my head. "Her family was rounded up and shot."

I sucked in my breath and nodded. I'd read enough Holocaust books to imagine how it happened, how the Nazis would have grouped them together, then shot them into a pit, like at Babi Yar. Did the Nazis play music while they killed them? Did they make them take off their clothes? I felt nauseous. "What about Grandma Rose?"

"She had already immigrated to Canada. Her Uncle Rafe had sent a ticket for her after he had settled here with his own family. He had promised to send for one of his brother's children."

I nodded. I'd heard the story of how she traveled by boat and then train. Grandma Rose's other siblings were all either older and married or too young to travel alone.

I'd stood up then, wavering. "I think I'll leave now."

Dad nodded and took a sip of his scotch. I saw him tilt his chair back as I left.

I went out to the garage and sat on the cold concrete floor and hugged a basketball in my arms. With a few rounds of ammunition, the Nazis had murdered most of Grandma Rose's family. Eleven people. Her sisters, parents, brothers, nieces and nephews, all shot. I'd seen a picture of Grandma Rose's sister Lydia, the two of them with lace ribbons in their hair. Not only was I named after Lydia, I had her nose too. When I looked closely at the picture, I could see I had her frizzy hair. I guessed I had her olive skin and black eyes too, but it was hard to tell from the picture.

I went outside and bounced the basketball under the maple in front of our house. A soft drizzle was falling. I tried to imagine my family being shot, what it would be like to have the Nazis arrive at my door and force me to leave. I imagined the sound of soldiers marching down our quiet, leafy street, soldiers ringing our bell. I froze in the driveway, clutching the basketball, and looked around. No one else was outside on this miserable, rainy afternoon. I tried to think about what it meant to be named for someone who had been killed. I shuddered and dropped the ball, letting it roll onto the lawn. Did Grandma Rose think of her sister every time she looked at me? It was hard to read Grandma Rose. She was so reserved, so proper and so…well, distant. Had she always been that way, or had losing most of her family made her like that? I couldn't imagine asking her.

I picked up the basketball and dribbled it to the end of the street and back, running under the tall maples. Then I dropped onto the front lawn, sweaty and out of breath. I could feel moisture seeping into my jeans. And why were they killed? Because they were Jewish. I didn't get that part. Dad had tried to explain it to me, but I didn't understand how following different laws and customs made people that different, or why the Nazis would care. I mean, I knew Hitler thought Jews were racially inferior, but it seemed so ridiculous to me. My Jewish friends weren't so different from my Christian friends. So we ate different foods and celebrated different holidays. Basically we were the same. Brooke, Chloe, Em, my Jewish friend Alexis and me—we all wanted a cute boy to like us, wanted to find the perfect pair of jeans and to escape our parents.

And yet, the Jews had always been persecuted. Most of the Jewish holidays were about different people trying to kill us. Passover was about the Jews being slaves in Egypt. At Purim, the Persians were after us. At Hanukkah, the Greeks tried to take over. Tisha B'av commemorated the loss of the temple, first to the Babylonians and then to the Romans. And let's not forget Holocaust Remembrance Day, marking the Nazis' destruction of European Jewry. At my house, every day was Holocaust Remembrance Day.

Who needed all this misery?

Why would anyone want to belong to a religion that was all about loss, grief and persecution? If I wanted misery, I could watch the evening news. Why couldn't I be part of a religion that focused on peace instead? Or at the very least, why couldn't Jewish holidays be like Easter and Christmas? Fluffy bunnies and Santa Claus, not death and persecution?

I looked at the sky. Dark clouds were moving quickly. I didn't want to be Jewish anymore. I didn't want to be part of a persecuted people.

That's when I decided not to be. It wasn't like my family kept many of the laws or traditions anyway. I would go to public school, change my name from Yanofsky to something like Richards or Smith and stop being oppressed by the Jewish holidays. It could be so easy. I could get my hair chemically straightened and get a nose job. No, wait— a nose job was as typically Jewish as Dad saying, *Oy*. I'd stick with my own nose.

I didn't want to belong to another religion; I just didn't want to be Jewish anymore. I didn't know a word for becoming un-Jewish, so I made up a list: de-convert, de-judify, de-Jew, de-religicize, de-belief, de-brief. I guess you could also say naturalize or normalize.

I tried to imagine a ritual for becoming un-Jewish. I could burn my bat mitzvah certificate, destroy Mom's collection of Yaffa Yarconi CDs, purge my parents' library of books about Jewish record holders, Jewish contributions to the atomic bomb, Yiddish jokes.

I never did any of those things. Instead, I refused to go to temple and Hebrew high school and Jewish youth group. When Mom threatened to cut off my allowance and Internet access if I didn't go to Hebrew high school or youth group, I said, "Fine" and started babysitting more and going online at Brooke's house. They finally relented when I went on my hunger strike.

And yet, even after I had started grade eight at public high school, I couldn't help thinking about Grandma Rose when I lay in bed at night, about her family being shot because they were Jewish. I remembered Grandma Rose crying on that stone, Dad trying to lift her up, the two of them locked in that hug. I wanted to forget I'd ever seen them. Six million dead Jews was a number too big to be meaningful, but the murder of eleven of Grandma Rose's family—my family—was like a fire ripping through my lungs.

Grandma Rose died a year after our trip to the cemetery. It was weird. One Friday night she was at our house for dinner, and she died in her sleep from a stroke that same night. My parents said it was the best way to go. I think they meant Grandma Rose was lucky she hadn't been shot into a pit.

Three

The weather starts to turn cooler, but the days are still bright and sunny. *Grease* rehearsals start—two lunch hours a week plus twice a week after school. Chloe is the lead dancer, and Em is playing Rizzo, the bad girl, which is ridiculous. Could there be anyone more like goody-goody Sandy than Em? The girl they picked for Sandy, Melanie Chan, does have a better voice and is in grade twelve, but *please*. Can't Mr. Matheson see that Em *is* Sandy?

Whenever Chloe and Em are free to have lunch with me, Brooke eats lunch with Chantal and Kelly. I can see her down the hall, laughing and whispering, but she doesn't even look my way. When she is around, Brooke acts like she's not doing anything new or unusual, but she smells like cigarettes.

It's weird. Chloe and Em fantasize about *Grease*, but the Smokers are *Grease*.

Mid-September, the Jewish holidays begin. The first is Rosh Hashana, the Jewish New Year. You eat apples dipped in honey and spend a long day praying in the overheated temple. Since most people don't show up for the service until after ten, I decide it's essential that I go to biology before services.

Mom is checking her email in the family room when I cautiously approach her the night before the holiday. "So." I clasp my hands in front of me. "I was thinking that since we're starting a new lab in biology tomorrow, I might go to class before temple."

Mom looks up from the screen. "On the holiday? I'm sure your teacher will let you make up the lab later."

"He would, no problem, but it's not like I would miss any of the service, and it would just be easier if I went. Also, the lab sounds really interesting."

Mom eyes me suspiciously. "You've never been very interested in science before."

I hold my gaze steady. "Biology fascinates me." This is not exactly true. I'm taking bio because I suck at chemistry, physics is bewildering, and I need a grade-eleven science.

Mom doesn't say anything for a minute, just keeps looking at me.

"I promise to help out with dinner in the afternoon." I know I sound desperate.

Mom narrows her gaze even more. "Fine. We'll be at school to pick you up at quarter to ten. Don't be late."

I scoot out of the room before she changes her mind. The real reason I can't miss biology is because Jesse is my lab partner. And he talks to me every day in class. He says, "How're you doing?" and I feel my cheeks heat up, and I say, "Good. You?" Sometimes I ask him how his weekend was, all the while knowing Brooke is listening, holding her breath, beside me. The day he asked me if I was going to try out for basketball this year, I thought Brooke might fall off her lab stool. It's weird—even though it's gorgeous Jesse, it's also just Jesse, the guy I used to have milk-chugging contests with.

When we'd started doing labs, I'd assumed I'd be Brooke's partner, but Jesse turned to me and said, "So how about it, Yanofsky? Are you getting the microscope, or do I have to?"

I was so flustered, I couldn't think of anything to say, so I just went and got the lab equipment. Brooke almost died of envy, but she seemed happy to work with Chantal.

In the morning my whole family sleeps in except me, and I leave for school early to avoid any conflict with Mom. I arrive in biology class feeling a little self-conscious, since I'm dressed in a skirt, sweater and tights instead of my usual yoga pants or jeans. Mom tried to buy me a gray suit, but I refused to even try it on. After Mr. Saunders explains the assignment, Jesse starts adjusting the lenses of the microscope. I sit quietly, pretending to study the lab sheet.

Jesse looks through the eyepiece of the microscope at a slide. "Hey, check this out."

I peer through the microscope. I'm so close, I can smell his spearmint gum. "Neat. It looks like a little swimming pool."

"Ah, simile." Jesse raises his hand for a high five.

I lightly hit his hand. "What?"

"You used a simile. The bacteria *is like* a swimming pool."

"You been studying for the poetry test?"

He nods and changes the slide. After peering through the microscope, he says, "Okay, look at this one. This amoeba is a fish."

"What? That makes no sense."

"Think like a poet. This amoeba is a fish. Get it?"

I stare at him blankly.

"It's a metaphor, Yanofsky."

I smile. "I think your metaphor sucks."

Brooke coughs, but I ignore her. I put another slide under the clips. "What does this one look like?"

Jesse leans over the eyepiece. "It just looks like bacteria." We laugh.

He sits up straight. "I'll give you another one." He looks at me intently. I try not to squirm. He is so unbelievably gorgeous, yet he still sounds like the old Jesse, like the person I used to know. It's exciting and unnerving at the same time. Jesse says, "Okay, I've got it. Your eyes are like— like cow patties drying in the sun."

"What?" My hands fly up to my cheeks.

"Simile. Your eyes are like cow—"

"I got it. Thanks."

"Wanna hear the metaphor?"

"My eyes are cow patties?"

"I bet you'll never forget metaphor and simile."

I wince at the touch of arrogance in his voice. "No, I won't." I look down at my biology notebook, hoping he'll quit giving me that smirk. I glance back. He still looks proud of himself. I don't remember him being so cocky. He probably knows how gorgeous he is. Still, he's looking at me differently now, and for longer. I'm not sure how to describe it, but it freaks me out.

Mr. Saunders calls the class back to attention, and Brooke passes me a note. I unfold it. It says, *WTF!!!!* I turn to sneak a glance at Brooke, but she pretends to be listening to Mr. S.

When I leave biology class, Mom and Dad are waiting for me in Mom's wagon. Zach's in the backseat, wearing his Batman cape and mask over his jacket and tie. It feels weird to be driving somewhere with my whole family on a weekday morning, and for a moment I feel excited by the uniqueness of the day. I used to love going to temple and having a day off school to play with my friends in the temple basement. I also liked the singing and the refreshments afterward. Now temple feels like a long boring ordeal where the prayers are interminable, the rabbi will ramble on forever, and I'll have to see kids I've been avoiding for the last four years. At least Alexis will be here from Seattle. She always comes up for the holidays to be with her grandparents.

Services have already begun by the time we arrive, and the congregation is reading a prayer in English as we enter the sanctuary. For most services, the temple is almost empty, but on Rosh Hashana and a few other holidays, it's so crowded that you have to reserve seats. Mom marches up to our row, waving at people and stopping to whisper hello. She has on a new suit and a giant eye-catching red hat. Even though Rosh Hashana begins the period where you pray to be forgiven for your sins and ask to be inscribed in this mythical Book of Life for the next year, some people, like Mom, use the occasion to dress up. I sigh with relief when we finally duck into our seats. Dad passes me a prayer book, and I open it to a random page and rest the heavy tome on my lap. Rabbi Birenbaum, who is the tallest, skinniest man I've ever seen, leads the prayers at the front.

Zach and I have nicknamed him the Specter. Poor Zach—his bar mitzvah lessons are supposed to be with the Specter, but I can tell Zach is terrified of him. Also, Rabbi B. has no idea how to talk to Zach. Most people don't.

The service drones on, Rabbi Birenbaum announcing the pages in English. I stand when everyone else stands, even say some of the prayers by heart, but otherwise I let my mind wander. Sometimes I find myself singing along, but then I stop myself.

Just as I'm about to die of boredom, it's time for the sermon. There's no way I can sit through Rabbi Birenbaum waving his huge skinny hands around for half an hour. As I stand up to excuse myself, Mom gives me a look, but I mouth "bathroom" at her and keep going. I scoot up the aisle to the main doors and sigh with relief as I head down to the washroom. Downstairs, kids are racing up and down the hallway, sliding on the soles of their fancy shoes. A clump of girls, including Rebecca Shuster, is gathered by the bathroom door. I hold my breath and sail past them without saying hello and take out my phone in a bathroom stall. There's a text from Chloe, You are the luckiest girl ever, and one from Em, I knew J had a romantic soul. A shiver of excitement courses through me. I take a moment to savor the memory of Jesse's attention, then check my hair and go look for Alexis. I find her waiting for me outside on the temple stairs, reading a fashion magazine. She's wearing giant sunglasses and exactly the kind of little suit Mom wanted me to wear.

Alexis and I have been best friends since nursery school. We went to Hebrew school together and were inseparable until four years ago, when her mom got this big administrative job at a hospital in Seattle. Since she moved, we talk on the phone, chat on Facebook and hang out whenever she comes back to Vancouver. Even so, we've grown apart. Alexis doesn't play sports, and most of the time when we hang out, we just talk. Last time Alexis visited, she brought her scrapbooking materials with her in a cutesy little hot-pink suitcase and spent more time talking to my mother about interior design than she did hanging out with me.

Alexis is on her school's cheer squad this year, which totally freaks me out. She says they do cool dances, but they also have to yell stupid chants. I'm sure Alexis looks adorable in her uniform because she's really petite and the white top would show off her long black hair, but cheer squad's main function is to cheer on boys' sports. Why aren't those girls playing the sports instead? It makes me want to barf. I've got a very long list of reasons why cheer squad is lame, but I'd never say anything to Alexis. Instead, I keep encouraging her to go out for soccer or track. She's a pretty fast runner.

Alexis and I give each other a long, tight hug and then I tell her about basketball camp and about sitting next to

Jesse in biology. Alexis asks me a zillion questions about Jesse and announces that I should ask him out. "It's not that easy," I say, and then I change the topic before Alexis can ask why not. Alexis is like that—she has a clear answer for everything, even when I just want her to listen and empathize. Alexis tells me about a film she's helping her boyfriend, Eric, make, and she gives me an update on cheer squad. I pretend to be interested because Alexis is my oldest friend, and even if we don't see eye-to-eye, I know we'll always be friends. Then Alexis says, "Eric and I are going to this Jewish youth-group convention in Portland in October. It'd be cool if you came too."

I frown. "Did my mom put you up to this?"

"No, I just thought it would be fun if you came."

"Fun?" I can't help smirking.

Alexis pulls her hair up and knots it on top of her head. "Look, if you're not into it, that's fine, but you don't have to put it down."

I try to make my face neutral. "Sorry. Yeah, well, I'll think about it." But I won't.

Alexis stands up, looking annoyed. "The sermon is probably over. I should get back."

"Oh, okay." I watch Alexis go into the temple, and then I sigh. Rosh Hashana is the time when you're supposed to ask people for forgiveness, not piss them off. I sit alone, enjoying the sunshine, for a few more minutes before I go back inside.

The service drags on. After the last few prayers, a series of announcements and a final psalm, it's finally over. Then I'm forced to wait for my parents to finish socializing. When we finally get home, I help Mom make chicken soup and *tzimmes* and cut vegetables for a *kugel*. Dad works on the turkey and stuffing, and even Zach helps by setting the table. He likes activities that create something orderly.

In the afternoon Mom and Dad take a nap before our guests come for dinner, and I sit down at the computer in the family room to do my homework. I decide to start with some research for a history paper on World War I. Mr. Whiteman said we could write about any aspect of the war that interests us. I hate it when teachers make essay topics so vague. What interests me about the First World War? Causes? Maybe. What if I wrote about the Jews in World War I? Right. I sigh and tell myself to get over the Jews. Maybe I should research civilian deaths. How did regular people—civilians—die during the war? I do a Google search on civilian deaths in World War I, and lots of articles about Armenia come up. Armenia? I don't even know where Armenia is. I do another search and find out it's near Turkey and that it was part of the Ottoman Empire. Okay, Armenian deaths in World War I it is. I start reading an article and am shocked to discover that between one and one and a half million Armenians were killed during the war. That's a lot of people. Then I read something so freaky it makes me sit up straight and curl my toes on the hardwood. The article refers to the killing of Armenians as *a holocaust*.

I stare at the screen. I've never seen the word written that way, with a lowercase *h*. Didn't *Holocaust* mean the killing of the Jews? Wasn't it a Jewish word?

I open a new tab and type the word *holocaust* into Google. Tons of articles about *the* Holocaust—the killing of European Jews by Nazis—come up. Huh. Then I search for a definition of the word. Turns out it's from the Greek word *holokauston*, which means "sacrifice consumed by fire." I go back to the article about the Armenians and scan through it, skipping the history section and focusing on how the Armenians were killed: deportation by forced marches, extermination camps, children killed by toxic gas. This sounds familiar enough to make my stomach clench. I lean back in my chair. Why is the killing of Jews during the Second World War referred to as *the* Holocaust while the extermination of over a million Armenians is only *a* holocaust? Is killing Jews more significant than killing Armenians? Armenians probably don't think so.

Maybe I'll write an essay comparing the two holocausts. No, enough with the Jews. I'll just write an essay about civilian deaths during World War I. I shake my head. Why can't I write an essay about changes in fashion during World War I, or the development of gun technology, or the draft? Why does everything always come back to the Holocaust? "I am my father," I say out loud, and then I shudder from my head to my toes. It could be worse though. I could be my mother.

I take out my history notebook and scribble: *The killing of Armenians was a holocaust.* Too general. What if I wrote, *The killing of Armenians during World War I was similar to the killing of the Jews in the Second World War?* Much better. I could jot down the outline right now. I shove the notebook back in my bag. I'm not supposed to be writing or even thinking about the Holocaust, *any* holocaust. I promised Alexis back in grade eight

It was Alexis who first realized I had a problem with the Holocaust. After the trip to the cemetery with Grandma Rose, I'd become obsessed with the Holocaust, even though I'd decided not to be Jewish anymore. It was weird: I was refusing to participate in anything Jewish, yet as I entered public high school, I started reading everything I could get my hands on about the Holocaust. And in my house, that was a lot. I read *Hana's Suitcase*, all the *Maus* books and Anne Frank's diary. Then I read books by Primo Levi and Elie Wiesel, and a novel by Susan Fromberg Schaeffer called *Anya.* I started going into Dad's study when he wasn't around and reading through his collection of Holocaust-survivor memoirs. I watched sections of the documentary *Shoah*, as well as all the popular Holocaust movies: *Schindler's List,*

Life is Beautiful, The Pianist, even *Sophie's Choice.* I couldn't seem to get enough. All through grade eight, Dad kept giving me more books, and sometimes we'd sit in his office and talk about them. He gave me background about the war in Europe and the Jewish effort to stop the Nazis. We ate from his secret stash of pistachios and talked about why Canada didn't allow more Jews to immigrate in the 1930s and '40s.

Alexis kept telling me I had to stop reading the books, that I was developing nervous habits like chewing my nails and pulling out my hair. She said I looked behind me a lot when we were outside.

One afternoon when Alexis was visiting from Seattle and we were walking to the 7-Eleven, the craziest thing happened. It was a crisp fall afternoon, and we were shuffling through the leaves in the gutter on my street when all of a sudden I remembered a dream I'd had, something about boots marching on a road. It wasn't very clear, so I stopped and tried to remember more of it.

Alexis asked, "What's going on?"

I stood still in the leaves. "I don't know." A flutter of terror crept over me. I couldn't move.

Alexis walked back to where I was, and the sound of her boots in the leaves triggered more memories of the dream, something about running.

"Omigod, I had this dream."

"Yeah?"

"Well, there were boots in it."

"Um…so?"

"I don't know, they were marching."

"And?"

"I'm not sure. I think they were chasing me." I looked at Alexis, trembling. I sat down on the curb and laid my head on my knees and wrapped my arms over my head. "I feel like I've been here before." Those boots had chased me down this street.

"Of course we've been here before. This is your street." Alexis crouched beside me. "You're acting really weird."

In my dream I'd been running, and men in high black boots were stomping after me, chasing me. As I remembered the dream, I felt my breath catch in my throat. I could hear Alexis asking me if I was okay. And I wanted to say something, but I couldn't. I felt like I wasn't properly anchored to the earth, even though I was sitting right on it, and in order to get re-attached and stop the jittery feeling coursing through me, I needed to hit something.

Alexis hunched over me. "Are you okay? Can you get up? You're really freaking me out."

"No," I said aloud. I wanted to sit and try to understand what was going on. I let Alexis haul me up, and that's when my heart started to pound like it was going to explode in my chest. I thought, Omigod, I'm having a heart attack and I'm only fourteen. It was crazy. I even had symptoms like in the ads on TV—the dizziness and the screwed-up vision.

The next part is really embarrassing. Alexis called my mom, who came and picked us up and took me to the hospital. The doctor checked my breathing and said I was fine, that there was nothing to worry about.

"I'm not fine," I said. "My heart is going to burst." I was shaking and trying to grind my fists into the examining bed.

The doctor said, "You're having a panic attack. Take some deep breaths and you'll feel better. I can show you some relaxation techniques to help you."

I wanted to go back to my street and bury myself under the leaves.

All the way home in the car, my mom kept asking me why I'd had a panic attack, and I kept telling her I didn't know. As soon as we got back from the clinic, Alexis and I went up to my room.

"You okay?" Alexis asked.

I nodded. I'd downed two extra-strength Advil in the bathroom when we got home, and my legs felt like Jell-O.

"I told you to stop reading all that Holocaust stuff. You're making yourself nuts."

I nodded.

"Listen, you scared the shit out of me today. I don't want you getting all crazy on me."

"I'm not crazy."

"I didn't mean it that way." She squeezed my hand. "I mean, I don't want you thinking all those negative thoughts. Anyone would be anxious reading about all that death and destruction." She ran her fingers along the shelf beside my desk. "Lauren, look at all these Holocaust books. Get rid of them. Read something else."

"Harry Potter?" I said weakly.

"Sure, or just read a fashion magazine."

I groaned.

I blew my nose, and then Alexis and I practiced one of the exercises the doctor had recommended: Five thoughts for the five senses.

"I see the blanket," Alexis said.

"I hear the wind," I said.

"I smell, um, I smell my shampoo."

"Okay, taste. I taste, well, my teeth."

"That's really pathetic."

"Well, I'm not tasting anything right now," I said. "You try thinking of a taste."

Alexis shook her hair out of her face. "I'm moving on. What's the next sense?"

I hit her with a pillow. "Feeling."

"Oh, right. I feel you hitting me with a pillow."

I hit her again.

"Ow, now I really feel it."

"The doctor was right."

"About you not dying?"

"Well, that too, but I meant about this exercise. It's very distracting."

"So's being socked in the head." Alexis swatted me with her pillow.

The next morning I took every Holocaust book off my shelf and stacked them in the corner of Dad's study, next to some boxes of books and files. I even added my Jewish Encyclopedia and some books about Israel, since they also mentioned the Holocaust. Back in my room, I rearranged the rest of my books and added some framed photos to the shelf to fill the empty spaces. I hid my Jewish prayer book at the back of my closet, so I wouldn't have to look at it. I should have gotten rid of it when I'd declared myself not Jewish at the end of grade seven.

Now I get up from the computer and call Alexis. I say, "I hope I didn't hurt your feelings earlier."

"Hey, no big deal. Different strokes for different folks."

I sigh. "I'm glad you feel that way. I wanted to ask you…"

"Ask me what?"

I think about the holocaust stuff, about asking Alexis what she thinks of the uppercase *H* versus the lowercase *h*, and the Armenians, but it would be such a long discussion. "Nah, I just wanted to hear your voice, make sure you weren't mad at me."

"Nope, not at all. Say hi to your mom for me."

For a moment I feel like asking Alexis to come over, so we can hang out the way we used to, but she's already hung up.

Four

The next day at lunch, Brooke is outside eating with the Smokers. Again. I'm hoping to eat with Em and Chloe because it's not a *Grease* rehearsal day, but instead of sitting down with their lunches, they head toward the main stairs.

"Where are you guys going? Do you have another rehearsal?" I ask.

"It's not that." Chloe twists her fingers together.

"What is it?"

"Well, we're going to check out Youth Alliance." Em looks at the floor.

"Oh. I see." I put on my best fake smile. "Well, see you." Like, never.

"Yeah, sure. Later," they say.

I sit on the floor with my lunch and watch Chloe and Em walk down the hall.

Youth Alliance is a Christian youth group that recently started at our school. I understand Chloe and Em going to dances on the weekend, or bowling and other youth-group things, but at school? Who wants to pray at lunch?

I totally don't understand Christianity. Chloe tried to explain it to me once. She said that Jesus was the Messiah and he died for everyone's sins. Even thinking about this makes me feel guilty. Everyone sinned and then Jesus died and then he forgave everyone for sinning? Chloe said that wasn't quite right. She did give me an explanation of the New Testament that I could understand. "Basically," she said, "be nice."

"Be nice? That's it?"

"Yeah, the New Testament is all about being nice to each other."

"Oh." I nodded. "I can go with that."

But not enough to show up at Youth Alliance and pray at lunchtime.

Nothing is worse than hanging out alone, but at least with a phone, you can appear less like a loser. I reach for my earbuds in my bag and curse Brooke under my breath. She should be here making fun of Christian youth group with me.

Across the hall, Mac, Tyler and their friend Justin are playing poker. With Jesse. He's been down our way more and more, hanging out with the basketball players.

I'm about to put in my earbuds when Jesse calls out, "Hey, Yanofsky, you want in?"

I freeze. Jesse looks at me expectantly. "Sure," I say. I slide my hair behind my ears and check the top button on my shirt. I feel myself starting to sweat. When I get some change from my coat pocket, I also grab a breath mint. Justin deals me in and I sit next to Jesse, our knees almost touching. I don't know Justin very well, but Mac and Tyler have been in some of my classes since grade eight. Mac's mom and my mom are friends, and Mac's had a crush on Chloe forever, so he's always hanging around.

I'm not great at card games, but I know how to play poker from basketball camp. So this is good, this is social, and I don't actually have to talk.

When the bell rings and Chloe, Em and Brooke all return to their lockers, the back of my shirt feels damp and I've lost five dollars, but it's worth every penny to see the look of astonishment on the girls' faces as Jesse and the others high-five me. "Hey, play again tomorrow?" Jesse asks me.

"Sure." I'll take cute boys over praying or smoking any day.

Jesse leans against a locker. "We'll have to play basketball again, so I can beat you."

I clasp my hands tightly behind my back. "Not likely."

Jesse pretends to shoot a hoop. "We'll see." Then he hip-checks me, hard enough to send me reeling sideways.

"Easy there, buddy," Tyler says to Jesse, grabbing my hand before I fall to the floor. I feel my face flush.

Back at my locker, I bury my burning face in my bag. Brooke elbows me and whispers, "You were playing cards with Jesse?"

"Poker," I say loudly.

"Wow, when did that start?"

"Well"—I turn and face her—"since you'd rather eat lunch with Smoker girls, I thought I better find some more friends too." Now I'm really sweating. I start walking toward the gym, leaving Brooke still digging for her running shoes.

"Hey, Lauren, wait up," Brooke calls.

I keep walking.

I ignore Brooke all through phys ed. We play volley-ball on opposing teams, and I try not to even look at her. All through history class, my phone buzzes in my pocket. I ignore it the first seven times, then take a peek when the teacher has his back to the class. Bathroom, Brooke's latest text says.

I don't go.

After school I don't wait for Brooke or Chloe or Em at the lockers; I just hurry out of the building. As I head for the field, I see Jesse playing basketball with Mac and Justin and some grade-twelve guys. I catch Jesse's eye, and he waves me over. I stop abruptly. It's cool outside, and I don't have my jacket zipped up, but I feel sweaty again. Great. Am I going to break out in a sweat every time I see a cute guy? That'll be attractive. I feel the nervous beat of my pulse as I head toward him.

"Hey, you should play with us." Jesse points back to the court.

I raise one eyebrow. "With the guys?"

Jesse bounces the ball. "Sure."

"You're all so much taller," I murmur. My phone buzzes in my bag, but I ignore it.

"Yeah, you are a bit of a shrimp now." Jesse lifts his hand up, showing off his reach. I make a face and stand up taller.

"Hey, Jesse, you in or out?" Justin calls.

Jesse looks back at the guys. "I'm in." He turns back to me. "I still want to take you on. One-on-one."

I think I might actually need to change my shirt at home. I start walking backward, away from Jesse. "Well, sure. Some other time." I feel my face burning again.

I stand and watch the guys play. Jesse is not the tallest, but he's definitely the cutest. And he moves down the court easily, like he's dancing. I watch him run his hands through his hair, pushing it out of his eyes. Mac says, "Dude, you're going to need a ponytail, like a girl." Then Jesse pulls a red terrycloth headband out of his pocket and shoves his hair back. Mac points and laughs, but Jesse says, "You wish you were cool enough for the headband." If only Brooke was here to see how hot he looks. Oh right, she's too busy with her new friends. I turn my buzzing phone off and bury it in the bottom of my bag.

Back at home, the landline keeps ringing. Mom has left me a flyer in front of the computer, about the youth-group convention that Alexis is going to. It promises a weekend of praying, singing, friendship and study. I rip it in half and shove it in the recycling bin. I spend a few minutes on Facebook, but the phone keeps ringing. I know it's probably Brooke, so I go up to my room, where I can't hear the phone. Eventually, Mom comes home from work, answers the phone and calls that it's for me. I reluctantly pick up.

"Hey," Brooke says, "I've been trying you for hours."

"Oh," I say. "I was busy."

"You're not mad at me, are you?"

"Well, no."

"Oh, good. You looked really pissed off at school."

"No, everything's fine. Great."

"I can't believe you were playing cards with Jesse."

I hear a hint of jealousy in her voice. I feel like saying, *We're going to play one-on-one, him and me, too.* Instead I say, "Yeah, well, it was no big deal."

"You keep saying that."

"You could have played too, if you were around." Even as I'm saying this, I doubt it. If Brooke had been there, I don't think Jesse would have asked me.

"I wanted to talk to you about that. Chantal's kinda having a hard time right now. Her parents are getting a divorce, and we're talking a lot about it. Also, there's this guy she's totally in love with. We have a lot in common."

"Oh."

"Anyway, Chantal and Kelly are going to a party at Dmitri's tonight. Want to come?"

Kelly is Chantal's best friend. She's a little overweight, with huge breasts that look like melons. She has dyed-blond hair and a smoker's cough, and she always wears bright red lipstick and too much eyeliner. Most of the Smokers, like Chantal, won't make eye contact with non-Smokers, but Kelly talks to everybody and even participates in class. She's like the Perky Smoker. I know her a little bit because she was on my geography project team last year. We did a study of cliff erosion at Towers Beach, which is right next to Wreck Beach, where people hang out naked. There were gross, wrinkly, old naked people right where we were taking soil samples.

I'm not sure what to say to Brooke about the party, so I ask, "Is Kelly still going out with Dmitri?" Dmitri graduated from our school last year but looks like he's thirty.

"Yep. The party will be fun. I'll ask my sister for some coolers."

"Well, I'm not sure…"

"Oh, come on, it'll be fun."

"Okay. I'll have to ask if I can go out." I know I don't sound enthusiastic.

"Tell your mom we're going to get coffee and study."

"Um, okay. What are you going to wear?"

"Jeans and a sweater."

"Okay."

I hang up the phone. I'm not entirely sure about going to hang out with the Smokers. It sounds like something I'm going to suck at. I think about calling Brooke back and telling her to forget it, but at least she's making an effort to include me.

When I'm ready to leave, Mom and Dad are sitting in the living room with the glass doors to the front hall closed. I open the door a crack. Mom looks exhausted, Dad frustrated. He's slumped on the white couch, his feet on the glass coffee table. I know from their conversation at dinner that Zach's bar mitzvah lessons started today and did not go well. His session ended with Rabbi Birenbaum chasing him through the sanctuary and Zach hiding under the stage in the auditorium. Mom had to leave work early to get him to come out, and now Zach is refusing to leave his room until they call off his bar mitzvah.

"I'm going out with Brooke for a while," I say.

"Be home by ten," is all Mom says.

Brooke and I ride our bikes to a house in Kitsilano and wheel them around back. A group of kids is hanging out on lawn furniture in the backyard, all smoking. I see Dmitri and Kelly and some other Smokers who graduated last year. There are some older guys too, friends of Dmitri's, I guess. Kelly waves to us, and Chantal turns around in her chair. She and Brooke exchange creepy air kisses, like they're old Mafia ladies. I hang back and wave hi.

Chantal's wearing leggings and a black sweater with a plunging neckline that shows off her cleavage. Shit, I think, I'm dressed all wrong. Everyone is wearing black, and I've got on my red hoodie, like I'm going to watch a football game. Brooke is wearing a charcoal sweater over a skimpy tank top and tight jeans.

Brooke pulls out coolers from her backpack, and we perch on a lawn chair together. Brooke and Chantal start talking in low voices about some guy Chantal likes who hasn't shown up yet. I pretend I'm part of the conversation.

I sip my sickly sweet raspberry cooler, take a deep breath and look around. Everyone is smoking. Brooke and I tried smoking last year in my back alley, but it made us cough too much. Besides, athletes shouldn't smoke. The guy sitting in the lawn chair beside me has blond curls poking out from underneath a ballcap. He looks like he might be twenty. Alexis says I should get over my fear of talking to guys, so I take a deep breath and say, "So, you think the Devils will win this year?" I point to the basketball logo on his ballcap.

"You like Duke?" he says.

I nod. "They're okay."

He sits up straighter. "Just okay?"

"Well, they're not North Carolina or UCLA."

"You sound like you know your stuff."

I shrug.

"Hey, check it out." He nudges the guy next to him with his foot. "A chick who knows college basketball."

I sigh inwardly and ignore the chick comment. I sip my disgusting drink and discuss my favorite players. I pretend to be interested in his fascination with Duke.

Then Brooke and Chantal get up. "We're going to the bathroom," Brooke says.

I feel like saying, "*So?*" or "*I don't have to pee,*" but I get up and join them. Chantal leads us into the basement and down a grotty hallway to a bathroom reeking of cologne. She leans against the sink. "I can't believe he didn't show," she moans.

I try to look sympathetic while Brooke hugs her. "Maybe he'll be here on the weekend," I say. "It *is* a school night." Could I sound any more like my mother?

Chantal ignores me and leans toward the mirror to apply more of her cherry-red lipstick. "But I'm horny tonight!"

Brooke sighs. "Me too."

I catch Brooke's eye in the mirror. We've never talked that way before. Brooke turns away from my questioning glance.

We walk back to the party and sit down. I blink twice when Brooke lights up a cigarette and inhales like she smokes regularly. The party continues around me, but I'm no longer in the mood to attempt conversation with random guys.

An hour later, after more smoking and beer, Brooke and I say goodbye and get on our bikes. "Thanks for coming with me," she says. We ride side by side down the quiet, leafy streets.

I shrug.

"So what did you think?"

"It was okay."

"Just okay?"

"Well, sure, you know, it was a party." It wasn't any different from the parties we'd gone to before—just people sitting around and drinking.

"It was much cooler than other parties," Brooke announces.

I'm saved from having to answer, because a car comes up behind us, and I fall back to let it pass. Was the party cooler because the guys at our parties usually play silly drinking games, or was it because the girls at our parties don't announce they're horny?

Brooke drops me off and I go inside, say hi to Mom and Dad, who are holding hands on the couch—talk about gross—and then head up to my room.

I lie in bed, looking at the streetlights creeping in around the edges of my blinds. My hair smells like smoke, and even after brushing my teeth, I still taste the cooler. Also, I can't get the sound of Chantal saying she's horny out of my mind.

The Perfects don't talk about their...I don't know. I'm not even sure what to call it—their desire? Lust? The Perfects talk about how cute boys are, or how in love they are. And they always fall in love with someone safely out of range. Em will say she's "maddeningly" in love with someone from her Bible class or drama troupe who is too old or dating someone else. Chloe shows no interest in any of the boys at school who salivate when she flounces down the hall. She only talks about her sister's older friends. Even Brooke's comments about liking men, not boys, put her safely in the same category as the rest of us. Since we only obsess over guys who will never acknowledge us, we'll never have to freak out about how far to go.

And me? Well, having a crush on Jesse is perfect. He is entirely in the realm of the impossible, not the actual. I can safely fantasize about him for the rest of high school and nothing will ever come of it.

And what if it did? What would that be like? What if we walked home from school together and then came down the lane behind our houses instead of down the sidewalk? We could talk simile and metaphor some more. I could come up with my own: your cheekbones are like ski slopes, your eyes are burning coals. You make me feel like a melting candle. What if he leaned me up against the back of the garage and bent down to kiss me? Shivers crawl down my spine as I imagine what his lips would feel like on mine, how his long arms would wrap around me and squeeze my back. I jolt up in bed. It'll never happen, not with Jesse. I can't even talk to him. I sigh, turn over in bed and pull the covers tight around me.

Five

The leaves turn red and yellow, then fade to orange and begin falling off the trees. I endure a long day at temple for Yom Kippur, the day of atonement, a holiday where you fast for your sins and ask God to forgive you for anything bad you've done in the past. Throughout October, Brooke continues to hang out with Chantal and Kelly, but one Saturday night she invites Chloe, Em and me over for dinner, just like old times.

When I arrive at Brooke's, Em and Brooke are making pizza and pretending to be on a cooking show. Chloe is videoing them with her phone.

"Ah, Signora Yanofsky, our guest taster, here to try the provolone." Brooke holds out a plate of cheese and Chloe pans the phone over to me.

I do my usual deer-in-the-headlights stare and say, "Very tasty," while shoving a large piece of cheese into my mouth.

"Ew," Chloe says. "Cut!" She pretends to be annoyed with me and then bounds into the living room and puts her phone in the speaker dock. She cranks up the volume, and we bounce around the living room. I follow Chloe's moves, even joining her in some surprisingly porny rolling around on the floor. This is the way it used to be: Brooke and Em doing their cooking show—"Now for another episode of the singing chef!"—and Chloe and me rocking out in the living room.

When the pizza is ready, Brooke carries it to the dining-room table. Then she brings a half-empty bottle of red wine. "Lookee, lookee, shall we start the evening with a little"—she reads from the label—"Chianti Classico? Ooh, so classy."

"None for me," Em says.

"But Em," Brooke says, swinging the bottle, "this isn't mere debauchery and drunkenness, this is an Italian cultural experience, compliments of my mother's latest boyfriend."

Em waves her napkin in the air and says, "Still, I think I shall not partake" in her poshest British accent.

Brooke shrugs and pours me a full glass. "Here, you're a lush. Drink up, babe."

"Thanks."

Brooke reaches for Chloe's glass. "Oh, that's okay," Chloe says, putting her hand over the top.

"What, you going all straightedge too?"

Chloe shrugs uncomfortably. "Sort of."

"That's retarded," Brooke says. She starts filling her wineglass and doesn't stop until it almost spills over the top. When she puts the bottle back on the kitchen counter, I hear her mumble, "Stupid Jesus freaks." She sits down at the table. "I bet you've even got a grace you're dying to share with us."

I look over at Brooke and scowl. I know Jesus isn't her thing, but does she have to piss off Chloe and Em? Chloe is frowning and looking down at her hands. Em looks concerned but composed, as always. She says, "Why, yes. As a matter of fact, I have the perfect grace. Yub-a dub-dub, thanks for the grub. Yay God!" She punches her fist into the air. Brooke and I stare at her. Chloe starts to giggle.

"Yay God?" I ask.

"Yep, yay God," Em replies. "Pizza, anyone?"

We all start eating. Brooke tells Chloe and Em about some Smoker party, but I'm not paying attention. Throughout dinner, as I drink all my wine and let Brooke fill my glass up again, I wonder, Do they really believe in God? They're intelligent people—surely they don't believe a divine force created the universe. I mean, there's science, people. There's no Sky Daddy up there saying,

Em and Chloe, you better be good girls. And think of the gazillions of wars, like the Crusades, that have been waged for religious reasons. Christians rode across Europe killing Jews to save Jerusalem from Muslims because they didn't believe in the one true God. That's insane. I consider asking, "What's the point in believing in God?" but we're finally all together, and I don't want to ruin the evening by alienating Chloe and Em. Besides, if you want to believe in God, I'm okay with that, as long as you're not using your religion as an excuse to kill other people.

Still, I feel a list brewing in my head. I think I'll call it "Reasons Believing in God is Stupid."

1. No one has any proof.

I'm about to list numbers two, three and four (evolution, the existence of evil in the world, how prayer doesn't work) when Brooke starts describing a sex act Kelly performed on her boyfriend using cough drops during a blow job. Totally gross, yet totally intriguing.

After dinner we walk to Quilchena Park to meet the guys. I'm excited because I know Jesse will be here tonight. I dressed carefully, wearing my lucky purple jacket and my favorite skinny jeans. It's a crisp night, without a hint of the usual fall dampness, so I'm not even worried about my hair.

When we get to the park, the guys aren't there yet, so we sit on the stairs by the washrooms. I tap my toes and sip from a water bottle full of orange juice and vodka, which I took from my parents' liquor cabinet after school, when they were still at work. Brooke keeps pulling out her phone and checking her messages.

"What are you looking for?" I ask.

"Chantal and Kelly said they'd be here tonight."

"Oh." Great.

In front of us, Chloe and Em practice a number from *Grease*. I pretend to watch while scanning the road for the guys' cars.

"*Summer days drifting away, to uh-oh*"—Chloe adds an emphatic pelvic thrust—"*those summer nights.*"

"*Tell me more, tell me more, was it love at first sight?*" Em sings in her clear, high soprano.

"*Summer dreams, ripped at the seams, but oh, those summer nights,*" they harmonize.

I clap when they finish.

"So," Chloe says, hands on her hips, "do you think Jesse will be here tonight?"

"Not sure." I feel Brooke tense beside me. I glance at her, but she's focused on her phone.

Em sighs. "If only he was playing Danny."

Chloe gives her a shove. "Back off, baby. He's Lauren's lover boy."

"Oooh." Em leans toward us and wiggles her fingers. "Lover boy."

Brooke stands up and pushes past them. "You guys are so lame."

Chloe and Em jump in the air and high-five each other. "Y-a-y lame!"

Brooke rolls her eyes, and Chloe and Em run across the park to the swings. I sip my drink, not wanting to get too drunk, just buzzed enough to keep the edge off.

I'm about to ask Brooke if she wants to go for a walk when a rusted old Toyota Corolla pulls up across the park. Five guys, including Jesse, pile out of the car. Then Mike Choi, the driver, pops the trunk and Tyler and Justin crawl out.

"They put people in the trunk?" I say. Mike only has his learner's permit, which means he isn't supposed drive without an adult in the car, let alone with people in the trunk.

Brooke just shrugs and calls out, "Hey!"

Justin waves at us.

We start walking down the hill to where the guys are dumping their backpacks and setting up lawn chairs. Suddenly, I feel a little drunker than I thought I was, as if my feet are farther away from my head than usual. I grab Brooke's arm to avoid stumbling as we head down the hill. More kids arrive, including some of the cast of *Grease*, and then Chantal and Kelly stroll up the hill, their cigarettes glowing in the dark.

"Hey, what's up?" Kelly says.

"Not much." Brooke shrugs. "You?"

"Nothing. Looking for a party. Heard people were meeting up here."

"Yep," Brooke says, "we're here." She points to Chantal's cigarette. "Can I have one?" Chantal silently hands her a cigarette and Brooke leans in and lights it off Chantal's cigarette as if she's been smoking all her life. Kelly holds out her pack to me. "You want?"

"Oh, no thank you." Jeez, I sound like a dork.

Kelly shrugs and puts her pack away, and I take a purposeful sip of my vodka. It tastes worse than it did earlier.

The four of us stand and watch the boys. Usually, we try not to attract the attention of passing cars when we're at the park. Tonight the guys seem louder, drunker, less concerned with keeping a low profile. Instead of lounging with their drinks and cigarettes, they are huddled together listening to Mike Choi.

"What are the drunken fucks doing now?" Kelly says. None of us reply. We watch Mike lift his hand to his forehead, yell something unintelligible and then sharply salute. The other guys salute back and then begin marching—no, goose-stepping—onto the field. I stare at them, my hands covering my mouth.

"What the hell are they doing?" Chantal says. We walk closer. Mike is explaining something, and as we approach, I can see they all have water guns. Not the big turbo kind, but little pistols that squirt at close range. Mike yells out some drunken command and half of the guys disperse, yelling and running into the trees around the edge of the park. I see Jesse loping across the grass.

"Oh," Kelly says, "they're playing war games again."

"Again?" I say.

"Yeah, they did it lots this summer. It's totally stupid," Chantal says.

"Guys are so useless." Kelly flips her hair. She and Chantal turn back toward the road. Brooke goes with them.

"I'll catch up with you later," I say, not bothering to check if they've heard me. I make my way closer to where Mike is standing with Mac and Tyler and some other guys, talking into his phone as if it were a walkie-talkie. I don't care that I'm alone and have no idea what I'll say to them. I keep walking until I can see their drunken grins, their slouchy jeans and black toques. Then I realize they're all wearing white armbands with Nazi swastikas on them. I stop and suck in my breath. Mike has his hand raised in another salute. "Heil Hitler," I hear him yell into his phone. Tyler gives a war whoop. Then Mike whistles with his fingers—one short, shrill cry—and the rest of the guys take off after the others, yelling and shooting their water pistols into the trees. I stand there, gawking. Mike says into his phone, "Can you hear me? Can you hear me? Report to command central. Over and out."

I'm still standing in the same spot, the guys streaming around me. What the hell? No, what the fuck? They're playing at being Nazis? I feel sick to my stomach. I want to run away, but where can I go? Brooke is smoking with Chantal and Kelly by the road. Chloe and Em are down by the swings, practicing their dance moves. Em is attempting an awkward cartwheel, and Chloe is doubled up laughing. I decide to dodge my way into the trees, not far from Mike. I squat in the damp grass and try to straighten out the thoughts snarling up my head.

Breathe. It's just a bunch of boys running around with water guns in a park at night, a stupid game. It's not like they're rounding up Jews or killing gay people. It's not like they care that I'm Jewish or even know that I'm here. But *still*. Nazis? How can they be so stupid? I feel panic start to rise in me, and I swallow it down. I don't have time for panic; I have to be clearheaded. I look out into the field. If I need to escape, I can sneak up through the trees to the old railway tracks and walk home from there.

It is very dark now and getting colder. I pull on my mittens and jam my hands in my pockets. Why aren't they pretending to battle Al Qaeda? I sit with my mouth open and watch Justin chase Tyler down the hill to get back to Mike without being squirted. Then Tyler trips, and Justin jumps on him and sprays him with his water pistol. I see Mac weaving through the trees, hunched over, looking behind him every few feet. I'm so intent on watching,

I don't notice anyone behind me until a voice says, "Hey, Yanofsky, is the coast clear?"

"Oh!" I jump up and turn around.

Jesse flicks a flashlight in my eyes. "Hah, I scared you."

"I didn't hear you coming." I'm still gasping.

Jesse playfully shoves me in the shoulder, and I push him back. He's wearing jeans, a red ski jacket and a black toque. His hair hangs over his eyes like a sexy eye patch. I realize I'm looking at him and not saying anything, but before I can open my mouth, Jesse grabs my arm and propels me in front of him and out from the trees. "Whaddya see?"

I swallow and try to compose myself. Jesse crouches behind me, still clutching my arm. I turn around and look at his beautiful face, then at the Nazi armband. The swastika is hand-drawn in black ink on white paper and held together with staples. Did they sit around making them while they drank? I feel the vodka churning in my gut. "So, whaddya see?" Jesse repeats. I peek around the tree. Mike has his back to us and is talking with Tyler and Justin. They are looking the other way, passing a beer back and forth.

"Am I good?" Jesse sounds impatient.

"Yeah."

He squeezes my arm and takes off across the field. He jumps on Mike's back and tackles him to the ground, squirting him in the head. Justin and Tyler fall down laughing.

I lean back against the tree and think about the pressure of Jesse's fingers on my biceps, the brush of his armband against my jacket. Then I hear Brooke calling my name. I come out from the trees and head toward the streetlight along the road. Brooke walks toward me. Kelly and Chantal stand by the road.

"Hey, where were you?" she asks.

"Oh, watching the guys. Did you see what they were—"

"Hey, Brooke," Chantal calls. "Are you coming?"

"Just a second." Brooke turns to me. "We're going to this other party at Kelly's cousin's friend's house. Do you wanna come?"

I look at Kelly and Chantal, posed with their cigarettes. "Nah, I think I'll hang with Em and Chloe."

Brooke shrugs. "See you later then."

I watch them head toward the corner. Behind me, the guys have emerged from the trees and emptied their water guns and are now drinking and laughing. They're still wearing their armbands. I don't want to be near them, so I walk to the swing set where Chloe and Em are still working on their dance routine, oblivious to the guys.

I watch them a moment as they cavort in the sand. It used to be the four of us on the swings.

"Hey, Lauren, we were looking for you," Chloe calls out. "We're going to DQ. Wanna come?"

I hesitate for a moment. I'm not up for more talk about Christian youth group or the play. I shake my head. "I don't think so."

"Okay, talk to you later," Chloe shouts at me. She and Em put their arms around each other and start waltzing toward the road.

"*So long*," Em sings.

"*Farewell*," Chloe calls out.

"*Auf weidersehen, goodnight*," they both shriek in falsettos. More giggles, more stumbling.

I stand, shivering, in the middle of the park, alone in the dark. The shortest way home is directly through the area where the guys are standing. I keep to the outside of the park instead, dodging through the trees and then breaking into a run at the hill. None of them glance my way, but I don't stop until I'm crouched in the tall grass on the tracks, with my hood over my head. I take a few deep breaths. I feel better, safer, hidden from the boys below.

I try taking more deep breaths to calm myself, but I'm too agitated. I need distraction. I turn and sprint up the road to my street and then down the sidewalk to my house, not stopping until I get to our garage, where I slam myself against the wall and try to convince my heart to stop thundering in my chest. I start counting breaths and then try to send each breath all the way down to my toes.

When I've calmed down a little, I pop some spearmint gum in my mouth to cover up any alcohol on my breath, walk around to the front of the house and let myself in. Mom is waiting in the front hall for me. "Where were you?" she says.

I jump. "God, Mom, you scared me." My pulse picks up again. "I was out with Brooke and Em and Chloe."

"And where are they?" Mom looks pissed off, like I've missed my curfew, even though it's only nine thirty.

"They went to DQ." I twist my fingers behind my back. "What's the problem?" I try to sound calm, even though I feel like I've had six cups of coffee.

Mom's lips tighten into a grim little line. "Justin Ferguson's mom called. She saw Justin getting into the trunk of Mike Choi's car, so she followed them to the park, where the kids were all drinking and smoking." She says *trunk* like it's a swear word.

I suck in my breath. "I don't know anything about guys in the trunk of a car." I try to concentrate on standing still.

"And the drinking?"

"Chloe, Brooke, Em and I were just there for a little while." I start to sweat in my jacket.

"Why were you in the park at night?"

"Oh, just hanging out." I take off my jacket and hang it in the closet, trying to act casual.

"At night? Since when do you girls hang out in parks at night?"

"Oh, we were only there for a bit, to meet up." I kick off my shoes.

"I don't want you hanging out in parks at night. It's not safe."

"Yeah, yeah, yeah," I mumble.

"Lauren?"

I turn to face her. "Okay. I heard you."

Mom sighs, and I head down to the basement, where I sit in the workshop and hug my knees to my chest. Maybe the boys just saw the Nazis on the History Channel and thought it looked cool or funny to goose-step. Maybe they don't actually know about the Holocaust, about what the Nazis did. I hold my breath for a moment and try to imagine this. Can there actually be people who haven't heard about the Holocaust? I try to imagine what it would be like to be a guy like Justin: white, male, smart enough, a good athlete, oblivious to genocide. His parents are still together, and he lives in a nice house near Chloe. What would it be like to grow up and only be part of regular culture: Christmas, Easter and Thanksgiving?

But what if the guys *do* know what the Nazis did? Maybe they think white supremacy is actually a good idea. Maybe next week's game will be about rounding up the geeks at school, or tormenting the Chinese kids. My heart starts going so fast, it feels like it's going to take off like a rocket. I try to focus on my breathing, but I feel like I can't get enough air. "Okay, this is just a panic attack," I whisper aloud. "I'm not dying." Still, tears form in my eyes, and I feel like smacking my fist against the wall to stop the building anxiety. I've had barely any panic attacks since that first big one in grade eight. The doctor said there were meds I could take if they got really bad, but I've always managed to calm myself down on my own. I force myself to think about five things for five senses. Okay, I feel the cold floor, I see the workbench, I smell the carpeting, and, um, my mouth tastes awful. Okay, what's the other sense? Right, hearing. Okay, I hear the hum of the furnace. I start over again. I feel the wall behind me, and I can hear leaves rustling outside. My mouth tastes vaguely of gum, and if I try hard, I can smell the paint cans. I keep going until I'm digging for smells and tastes and I've distracted myself from the boys and their armbands. My breathing slows. I'm not dying of a heart attack at sixteen. Then I start to feel sleepy and sore from sitting on the cement, and I get to my feet and go up to my room. I brush my teeth and pull on my favorite flannel pajamas with stars on them and get into bed. Only by imagining lanterns at the festival am I able to calm down and then finally sleep.

Six

The next morning I sit up slowly and drink a glass of water. The backs of my eyes ache and my head pounds, as if drums are being played in my skull. Alcohol is so not worth it. I roll over and think about the guys' armbands, then feel myself shudder. Who can I talk to about this? I hesitate before dialing Alexis. She'll freak, but I need to tell someone. Her phone rings three times before she picks up.

"Hey, Lauren." She sounds sleepy.

"Did I wake you?"

"No, but I'm still in bed." She yawns. "What's up?"

"I have something crazy to tell you, but I don't want you to overreact. And you can't tell anyone."

"Is it about that guy, Jesse?"

I hesitate. If I tell her the truth, then how can I still like him? "No, it's not about Jesse."

"Oh, too bad. I thought you were going to tell me something juicy."

"No, I was at a party last night. Well, not a party, exactly. Just some kids hanging out at the park."

"Oh yeah?"

"Well, the guys...they were playing this war game, this Nazi war game."

"They were WHAT?" I imagine Alexis sitting bolt upright, wide awake.

"I know. It was nuts. They were wearing these Nazi armbands, yelling *Heil Hitler!* and pretending to shoot each other."

"Who? Who?"

"Oh, just some guys from school. You don't know them."

"Omigod, that's crazy. What were they thinking?"

"I—I don't know."

"And these guys are your friends?"

"Well, sort of. We hang out with them at school."

"Wow, that's crazy. What are you going to do?"

"I dunno."

"You have to tell someone," Alexis announces.

I groan. "Tell who what?"

"I don't know. Your parents or the school. They can't make fun of what the Nazis did."

"I'm not sure telling someone is a great idea."

"Lauren, it's not an option. You have to tell. It's anti-Semitism."

"But if they don't know the Nazis killed Jews, is it still anti-Semitic?"

"That's beside the point. You have to tell someone."

"Well, um, I'll think about it."

"Promise?"

"I said I'd think about it. Anyway, I should go now."

"Hey, what about that Jesse guy?"

I freeze. "What about him?"

"You guys still talk?"

"Sometimes."

"Oh, that's good. Text me later."

I put down my phone and roll over in bed. Tell someone. Yeah, right. Fat lot of good that would do. People would get all upset about anti-Semitism and talk about how the Holocaust could happen again anytime. Alexis can get very worked up about hate crimes against Jews, none of which seem to be happening anywhere near us. It's true that Jews were treated like crap in Europe for centuries, but things in North America look pretty good for Jews these days. I know you can still find Holocaust deniers and people claiming that Jews drink Christian baby blood, but you can also find people who say the earth is flat and global warming is a myth. Besides, in our own lives, in Canada, none of that anti-Semitic stuff is happening—not like in the past anyway. Now Jews own land, join country clubs and attend any university they like. People get riled up about Israel, but to my mind, that's political, not religious. The guys at school are idiots, but anti-Semitic? I think not.

My phone beeps. It's Brooke. B-fast? she texts.

I write back, Benny's?

Meet here.

In an hour.

I shower and put on jeans, a pink long-sleeved T-shirt and a pair of silver flats.

I wheel my bike out of the garage and inhale the crisp fall air. A few leaves are still on the trees, shining in the sunlight, but there are lots to crunch on the edge of the road. One of my neighbors is out raking, and I feel like jumping into the pile of leaves like Zach and I used to do.

I want it to be just another beautiful fall day, but it isn't. It's the day after the guys pretended to be Nazis. The Holocaust is truly unavoidable. If it's not boys playing Nazi in the park, it's news on the car radio about Holocaust survivors or stolen art or reparations or a new museum or monument. If I go to the library and look at a list of books for Jewish teens, most of the books will be about the Holocaust.

But worst of all, the Holocaust is in my head.

I bike along the road, listening to the leaves crunch under my tires. Down the street, I see Jesse playing basketball in his driveway. I slow down and think about turning back, but then he waves at me. I freeze for a second and then bite my lip and bike toward him.

There has to be some good explanation for the Nazi stuff, right? Maybe he'll apologize if I tell him how offensive I thought it was. Or maybe he'll say he had no idea who the Nazis were or what they did. One of those has to be the case.

Jesse is dribbling the ball. "Hey, Laurensky, wanna shoot hoops?"

I twirl a lock of hair around my fingers. "I'm supposed to meet Brooke and"—I look down—"I don't exactly have the right shoes." I'm not wearing a sports bra, either, but I don't mention this.

Jesse winks at me and does a layup. "Oh, well, if you're too scared…"

The ball bounces off the rim, and I grab it as it rebounds off the pavement toward me. "Fine. I'll take you. Ten minutes max." I pass him the ball and get off my bike.

I walk toward Jesse and stand facing him. I can feel my blood pounding in my temples. Jesse looks down at me—he's a full head taller than me now—and grins. The scent of his deodorant makes it hard to concentrate. "You ready?"

"Wait." I knot my hair at the nape of my neck.

He dribbles the ball and goes in for a layup. I try to block him, but my shoe falls off. Jesse scores. I swear under my breath. "Nice one," I say.

He passes me the ball. "You start."

I dribble for a moment, then kick off my shoes and look up at him. The driveway is cold under my bare feet. Jesse has a look in his eyes like nothing matters, like everything is easy. I know he can easily block me, so I have to be faster, smarter. I jab-step right, cut left and pull up for a quick shot. I'm a little outside my range, but the ball arcs and swishes through the net. I cross my arms across my chest as I land on the ground, holding my boobs in tight.

Jesse catches the ball on the rebound. "Not bad, for a girl."

I feel myself turn red, and I slap the ball away from him. "Hey, whatcha doing?" he says.

"Playing like a girl," I say and shoot again. I miss this time, but my next shot goes in. We play hard for another ten minutes. I may be quicker, but Jesse and his long arms roundly defeat me, 11-8. He slaps me on the back. "Good work." Then he goes into the house for water and comes back with two plastic sport bottles. We sit on the curb and drink.

"You been practicing?" he asks.

"Basketball camp."

Jesse swigs from his water bottle. "I thought you went to some Jewish camp."

"I haven't gone there in a couple of years."

"How come?"

"Not enough basketball. Too many war games, stuff like that."

"Sounds like fun."

"It's not my thing. Actually, I wanted to talk to you about war games."

"Oh yeah? What about them?"

"What was going on last night?"

"You mean the park thing?"

"Yeah, the park thing."

Jesse gives me a big lazy smile. "That was fun."

I hug my arms across my chest. "Pretending to be a Nazi is fun?"

"Oh that. Yeah, that was fun—a joke."

"The Nazis killed millions of people, and you think it's fun to pretend to be one?"

"Oh, c'mon. We weren't really being Nazis. It's not like we were playing concentration camp. I mean, I know about all that crazy shit. We were just a bunch of drunk, stupid guys running around a park with water guns. No harm done, right?" He punches me lightly on the arm.

I stare at him incredulously. "Are you serious?"

Jesse holds up his hands. "It wasn't my idea. When I got to Mike's house, the guys were already making the armbands."

"And you had to follow along?"

"Aw, don't be like that. It was, like, instead of playing video games where we try to kill stuff, we were outside trying to kill each other. It was good times."

I sigh. "Why couldn't you be an anti-terrorist squad, or pretend to bust drug runners, or...I don't know— be cowboys and Indians?"

He squints at me. "Is that really any better?"

"To me it is."

"Well, there you go. This is all about you."

"How could it not be? I mean—Nazis?"

He shakes his head and downs the rest of his water. "You need to relax."

My mouth falls open. "Relax?"

"You know, just chill. Don't take everything so seriously."

I think of Grandma Rose on the stone, sobbing, Dad trying to hold her up, my eleven murdered relatives, and I wonder how I'm not supposed to take this so seriously. I stare at Jesse, knowing he's waiting for me to say something. I want to say, *You don't know shit about me*, but what's the point? I start backing away. "Basketball was fun. We should do it again. You know, with shoes and all. And thanks for the water." I put down the sports bottle and pull my hair out of its knot.

"Hey, Lauren, you're not really pissed, are you? 'Cause you know I didn't mean to hurt your feelings." He rubs his knees. "Aw shit, I'm sorry."

"No, it's okay. It's fine. I'll see you around." I get on my bike.

"Hey, wait."

"I gotta go."

I cycle down the street and turn the corner, heading toward the park. I can't believe it. What an idiot. I need to relax? I knew he was too cocky.

I stop to wait for the traffic light to change. Just when I think I can be normal, the Holocaust reappears in my life and makes me Jewish again. How pathetic is that? Couldn't I be outraged because the Nazis killed millions of people? I am. But mostly I care because the Nazis killed eleven people in my family. *My* family. I bang my fist on the handlebars. "My life is so stupid," I say to a maple tree.

Brooke is waiting for me on her front doorstep with her bike. "What took you so long?"

"Hair."

"Oh."

We get on our bikes and ride to Benny's Bagels, where we both order tea and a bagel with peanut butter and honey and then take our food up to the balcony.

"So where did you go last night?" Brooke asks.

"Just home. After I saw the guys' war games, I…"

"Guys are dumb." Brooke sighs and sips her tea.

"Did you see the armbands they had on?"

"With the swastikas?"

I nod.

"Superbad taste."

"It freaked me out." I shudder and grip my mug.

"Oh, they were just being drunken idiots. They play all those war video games and then they get shit-faced and need to burn off some of their testosterone by pretending to shoot each other."

"I can't believe you'd say that. They were pretending to be Nazis. That's fucked up."

Brooke flips her hair. "Like I said, superbad taste, but they weren't serious. I wouldn't get all worked up about it."

My breath catches in my throat, and I stare at Brooke like it's the first time I've seen her. I look at the barrette holding back her long bangs, at the freckles on her nose, the thin blond hairs on her forearms. I can't believe she's saying this. "You're as bad as Jesse."

"What do you mean?"

"He said the same stupid crap."

Brooke sits upright. "You talked to him?"

"Yeah, he was playing basketball in front of his house this morning. We played a little one-on-one." Brooke's eyes have opened really wide, but I'm still thinking, Brooke doesn't get it. She doesn't think the guys' game was a big deal. Even though she's seen the picture of Grandma Rose's family in my room and asked who they were and I told her how they died, she still doesn't get it.

Brooke grips the table edge. "Omigod. You played basketball with him?"

"Don't get too excited. He's a lot more arrogant that he used to be."

"Does that mean you wouldn't go out with him?"

"Well…" I pause, thinking about the way he teased me and how good that felt. "How could I? I mean, he was pretending to be a Nazi." I shudder.

"Does this mean you wouldn't mind if someone else went out with him?"

My toes curl up in my flats. "What do you mean?"

"I mean, what if one of your other friends was interested in him?"

"And they didn't care that he thought pretending to be a Nazi was okay?" A heaviness settles over me, and I feel like I can't move in my chair.

"Well, no. Say they knew it was wrong and all, but if someone else had a crush on him…"

I hesitate. "I guess anyone else could have a crush on him. I'm sure half the girls at school are in love with him." I'm having trouble concentrating on what Brooke is asking me because my brain is still processing that Brooke doesn't care that Jesse dressed up as a Nazi. Did anyone at the park last night care? Am I the only one who thought it was wrong?

Brooke leans forward over the table, resting her chin in her hands. "Okay, I have to tell you something, but you have to promise not to be mad."

"Oh." I bite the inside of my cheek. It's never a good sign when someone makes you promise not to get mad.

"Do you promise?"

"Well, um, sure."

"Okay, I didn't want to tell you, because I knew you were interested in him, but, well, I really like Jesse."

"Oh."

"You're so mad at me, aren't you?"

"Oh, well, I..."

"I didn't want to tell you, but Lauren, it's not just a crush. I've liked him ever since he came back to school last year."

I grasp my mug and grind the toes of my shoes into the floor. I'm not sure what to say.

"I mean, I think I would die for him. Like lie down in traffic or take a bullet." Brooke's eyes are sparkling, and her cheeks are glowing like she's gone for a run. I've never seen her like this, not even when she won MVP last year.

"Oh, wow."

"And that's why I haven't been hanging out with you, because I didn't think you could understand, and Chantal and Kelly did."

"Oh, wow."

"You keep saying that."

"I'm not sure what else to say." I grip the sides of my chair, my ankles tightly crossed. I'm not even sure what to think.

"Well, you could say it's okay for me to go out with Jesse."

I dig my fingernails into the palms of my hands. Can I say, *Yes, I still want Jesse even though he thinks it's okay to dress* up like a Nazi? Do I say, *No, I'm going to have a shit fit if you go out with him?* Finally I mumble, "I'm not sure what to say."

"'Cause if you don't want me to, I won't go for him." Brooke looks at me expectantly. My eyes dart to the side for a moment, as if I'm hoping someone will come along and interrupt our conversation and I won't have to respond. No one comes, and when I look back at Brooke, she's still looking at me like she's a hungry dog and I'm a hamburger.

"Well," I say slowly, "I guess—I guess if you want to ask out a guy who thinks dressing up as a Nazi is no big deal, then that's your..." I want to say *problem*, but I settle for, "I guess that's for you to decide." I'm trying hard to keep the bitterness out of my voice. I look at my watch. "I need to go." I stand up and pull on my jacket.

"Shit." Brooke runs her hands through her hair. "I knew you were going to be so mad at me."

"No, it's okay. You really like him, and I guess the Nazi thing's not so problematic for you."

Brooke looks up. "What's that supposed to mean?"

"Did your family get killed in the Holocaust? I guess not. Neither did Jesse's. You and Jesse will be perfect for each other." I get up and run down the stairs, leaving Brooke alone in Benny's. Out on the street, I sit on the curb by my bike and squeeze my head in my hands.

My phone beeps.

Don't b mad, Brooke texts.

I write back, ok.

U still mad?

No.

Want to ride tog?

No.

Call later?

Maybe.

Nazis suck.

No shit, I think. I shove my phone in my pocket and get on my bike.

Seven

At home I curl up on the wicker couch in the kitchen and pull out *The Color Purple,* the book I'm reading for English, to distract myself from thinking about Brooke. I'm surprised I like a schoolbook so much. Most of the stuff I have to read for English is about boys or old men, but *The Color Purple* is all about women. Just as I'm settling in, Dad comes in with a bag of chips and a stack of books.

"Hey, Laurensky, whatcha reading?"

I hold up the book and hope he'll leave me alone.

"Ooh, feminist stuff, huh? I have something you might like." He shifts through his stack and pulls out a book with a yellow Star of David on the cover.

I shrug my shoulders. "I think I've already read that one."

"No, this is new. It's the story of a young girl who survives—"

I put up a hand to stop him. "Let me guess. It's about a girl who gets sent to a concentration camp. The Nazis gas the rest of her family but keep her to do forced labor. She has to eat crappy food, and she has no shoes. Everyone around her dies of horrible diseases or starves. She survives, but when she tries to go home, other people are living in her house." I'm sitting up now, clutching my book. "And then she finds out"—I swallow because my voice is getting shrill—"that all the Jews in her village and in the villages nearby are dead."

Dad stands by the stove, staring at me, dumbstruck. I take a deep breath. "I don't need to read any more Holocaust books, Dad. I could write my own if I wanted to."

"Oh." Dad leans on the counter, still staring at me.

"Was I right? Is that the story?"

"Well, sort of. It's about a survivor who meets her childhood sweetheart years after the war, in Israel, and falls in love all over again."

I narrow my eyes. "But it's also about how she survived, right?"

Dad fans through the pages. "Well, yes."

"See? Same story, just a different ending."

"Aha!" Dad jabs a victorious finger in the air. "But the ending is what counts. It's all about hope."

I stare at him bleakly. "All that death puts a bit of a dimmer on any hope, for me. Besides, I don't read Holocaust books anymore."

"Since when?"

"Well, since right now." I'm lying, of course.

"Oh, I didn't know that."

"Well, now you do. I'm done with the Holocaust. I don't want to ever read another Holocaust book, see a Holocaust movie, hear a Holocaust anecdote or meet another survivor. As far as I'm concerned, I know enough."

"Oh. Do you have to be so definitive?"

"Yes."

"So, what are you going to read?"

I hold up my novel. "Maybe I'll read about the oppression of women. That could take a lifetime."

Dad shakes his head and holds out the Holocaust book. "You sure you don't want this?"

"No, and if you invite any more survivors to dinner, I'll be out."

"Okay then." Dad stares at me some more. Then he holds out the bag of Doritos. "Chip?"

"No, thanks."

Dad shrugs. "More for me then." But he doesn't sound like his usual joking self.

I get up and head to the computer.

I could have described the horrors of the concentration camps in more detail for Dad, but enough of that. I sign on to the computer and open a new document. I have a new list in mind.

Ten Ways to Stop Thinking about the Holocaust:
1. Straighten hair.
2. Sprint uphill.
3. Fantasize about Jesse.
4. Recite times tables.
5. Think up lantern ideas.
6. Play basketball.
7. Write lists.
8. Learn about different atrocities.

What I didn't tell Dad was that even though I've been trying to avoid the Holocaust ever since grade eight, I still can't get away from it. Sometimes it feels like a cloud of smoke constantly blowing in my face. Sometimes it's obvious, like my writing a paper on Armenian genocide. That's my own fault. But other times, it's totally random. Like the time Alexis and I asked if we could get tattoos—little flowers on our ankles. Alexis's mom said, "One day you might have a job where you'll have to wear panty hose, and a tattoo might look unprofessional. Or you might be allergic to the dye, and those needles might not be clean."

My dad said, "Did you know they tattooed numbers on people's arms during the Holocaust?"

I wanted to say, *It's just a flower on my ankle, and I'm choosing to do it*, but I didn't. How do you argue with the Holocaust? You don't.

And it's not just me and my little world that are overrun with Holocaust stuff. When I went to the library last week to get books for my Armenia paper, there were a few books about the Armenian genocide, but shelves and shelves about the Holocaust. One website claimed that in one year *The New York Times* printed more articles about the Holocaust than about all of Africa. That made my arm hair stand up. I wondered why there was still so much Holocaust stuff out there compared to everything else. The website's claim made me nervous. It made me think of the accusation that Jews control the media. Which isn't true. And it's anti-Semitic to think that way, right?

For dinner, Mom makes lasagna and a salad. Zach's wearing his Batman gear at the table again and doing this toe-tapping thing he does when he's agitated. Zach's been wearing the Batman outfit more often since the trouble started with his bar mitzvah classes.

"So," Dad turns to Mom, "Lauren told me something very interesting today."

"What's that?"

I spear a lettuce leaf and pretend to ignore him.

"She told me she isn't reading any more Holocaust books."

"I'm reading *The Color Purple*," I say to Mom. "It's amazing."

"My book club did that one a couple of years ago," she says.

"Anyway," Dad continues, "the book I wanted Lauren to read isn't really a Holocaust book. It's about hope and the future of the Jewish people."

"That sounds interesting," Mom says.

I focus on cutting the lettuce leaf into smaller bits. "This is a great salad, Mom."

"New dressing," she says, "with dill and a touch of maple syrup."

"I'm still curious," Dad says. "Why the sudden moratorium on Holocaust books?"

I put down my fork and sigh. "You're not going to let it go, are you?"

"I'm curious, that's all."

I take a deep breath. "Well, I guess I'm sick of hearing about Jews being killed. You'd think we were the only people who were ever massacred."

"Aha." Dad points with his fork. "The Holocaust was different because it was the first time technology was used to systematically kill people." Dad has the annoying look on his face he gets when he thinks he's winning a good debate.

I put down my fork. "You think the Turks didn't have weapons when they killed the Armenians? That's a form of technology."

"What's this about the Armenians?" Mom asks.

"You see? Mom doesn't even know about the Armenians. But everyone knows about the Jews."

"What's your point, Lauren?" Dad asks.

I feel my skin heating up, and I grip my fork. "I think the Holocaust is way overdone. I think people should move on. Forgive and maybe also forget, focus on something else."

Dad isn't smiling anymore. "That sounds pretty dangerous."

I throw up my hands in frustration. "Great. We get to obsess about the past forever. Sounds like fun." I get up from the table and clear my plate as quietly as I can, but my hands are shaking and I accidentally slam the dishwasher door, rattling the china. Both of my parents cringe. "Sorry," I say, "and thanks for dinner, Mom."

I leave the kitchen and stand in the front hall, trying to decide whether to run down the street or go up to my room. I hear Dad telling Mom about the Armenians. He uses the word *genocide* instead of *holocaust*, and I want to go back into the kitchen and argue with him some more.

Instead, I hide in the upstairs bathroom with my back against the door.

When I calm down, I force myself to sit at my desk and do my biology homework and then some reading for history. It's a relief to concentrate on something other than Brooke or Jesse or the crazy conversation with Dad. When I finish my homework, I head down to the kitchen for a snack. Beside the fruit bowl is the stack of books Dad was showing me earlier. I can't help flipping through them as I eat yogurt. There's one on the Warsaw Ghetto uprising and another about the Righteous Gentiles—people who saved Jews—in France. Another is about stolen art. I flip through the glossy pages to see the paintings. I pick up the book Dad wanted me to read. It has a black-and-white photo of a young couple on the front cover and a color photo of an ancient couple on the back. I read the book jacket. It sounds like the kind of book I'd like, not so much for the middle bit about death and destruction, but for the part about how they were reunited in Israel. No. I put the book down. It isn't good for me to read this stuff. I need to keep my mind clear.

The last book in the stack also has black-and-white photos on the cover. I look closely and realize they're all twins. I feel my breath catching in my throat. Yeah, Hitler probably killed cute little twins too. I swallow the tickle in my throat. But it isn't a book about just any twins: it's about Mengele's twins.

I know Mengele was a creepy doctor who did weird medical experiments on concentration-camp prisoners, but I don't know about the twins. I read the front and back covers, then sit down on the floor by the heating vent and read the introduction. The book is about the horrible experiments Mengele did on twins. I know I should stop reading. I'll make myself sick again. I promised Alexis I wouldn't read this kind of thing, but I can't stop. It's like I'm addicted to the details, no matter how horrifying.

I take the book upstairs with me and brush my teeth and put on my pajamas. Then I climb into bed and continue reading, even though I'm tired and I want to stop. I have to read each detail so that maybe one day I'll understand how such evil could exist in the world.

It gets very late, and everyone else has gone to sleep. I am still reading, skimming for the most horrible parts. I read until my eyes ache, until my shoulders cramp from holding them so tight. Mengele chopped people up without anesthesia. He tried to make Siamese twins by sewing them together. Sometimes he did experiments on one twin and not the other, and one twin died. Most of his victims died from infection. I can feel my back tightening, my jaw locking, as I read. I can't stop reading until I come to a section on experiments he did on women's reproductive organs, how he made them sterile. Reading about Mengele doing stuff to women is way too freaky. I slam the book shut and shove it under my bed.

I lie on my back in bed, my body stiff, my mind humming with an aggravating buzz. I try to remember being at the lantern festival, being surrounded by those paper-bag lanterns. In my mind I lie down on the grass, encircled in flickering light. Nothing can harm me here, not even scary thoughts. I imagine myself protected by light and slowly calm myself down until I drift to sleep.

Eight

On Monday morning I shower, moisturize, blow-dry my hair and then discover my straightener doesn't work. I push the on-off switch a dozen times, but the little red light won't come on. This is a disaster of the highest order. My hair is a giant poof of poodle frizz. I swear and smack the straightener down on the counter.

Dad knocks on the door. "What's up?"

"Hair issues."

"Make a ponytail and call it a day."

"It doesn't work that way!" I try French braids, but my hair looks lumpy, and frizz starts to erupt through the braids almost instantly. I try adding a hair band, then rip it out and throw it against the door. I need the straightener.

Zach bangs on the bathroom door. "Hey, I need to pee."

"Fine." I yank my hair free of the braids, get back into bed and pull the covers over my head.

Mom knocks on the door. "Aren't you getting up?"

"I can't. The straightener died."

"Oh, how bad is it?" I pop my head out; hair is springing around it. "Oh. Not so bad."

I pull the covers back over my head. "You're a terrible liar."

"I see. Well, how about a hat?"

"You have to take a hat off inside school."

"I see."

I think I might kick her if she says that again. "Could I please get it chemically straightened?"

Mom sighs. "I'll see what I can do." She leaves the room and I hear her making breakfast for Zach, and then the car pulls out of the driveway. The house is quiet.

Okay, so it's not just my hair. It's Jesse the Nazi. And Brooke the traitor. What the hell am I supposed to do? Ignore the game and hope the boys don't play again? Rat them out and hope they get in trouble?

Mom comes back twenty minutes later with a straightener in a plastic bag.

"Where did you get it?"

"I borrowed it from Shayna Shuster. Rebecca doesn't use it much."

I make a face. She raises her eyebrows. "Shayna says it gets really hot, so don't burn yourself." She checks her watch. "If you hurry, I'll drop you off at school."

"Don't you have to be at work?"

"I cancelled my nine fifteen."

"Oh, thanks."

"I understand hair. Do you want me to take you to get a new straightener after school?"

"No, that's okay. I can walk up to London Drugs myself."

"Fine. Put it on your debit card, and I'll pay you back." Mom gets up to leave. "Do you want a bagel to eat in the car?"

"Yes, please, with cream cheese."

Sometimes Mom is all right.

It's a raw, wet day, the kind where the rain seems to fall sideways and the dampness gets into your skin. Mom wears one of those plastic old-lady rain kerchiefs over her hair to walk from the house to the car. "You've got to be kidding," I say.

"I wouldn't say a word about frizz, if I were you."

I close my mouth and get in the car.

I'm late for biology. Mr. Saunders takes my late slip and nods for me to sit down. I don't dare look at Jesse or Brooke. As soon as the bell rings at the end of the period, I hustle out of class. Even so, Jesse catches up to me in the hallway.

"Hey, what's the rush?"

"Nothing."

"Nothing?"

"I'm going to English."

Jesse grabs my shoulder. "Hey, c'mon, I apologized."

"Yeah, thanks." I stop a moment and look at him. He looks genuinely sorry, and I don't know what to say. "I have to go." I pull away, holding the shoulder he touched.

At lunchtime Chloe, Em and I walk to the convenience store for chips. When we get back to our lockers, Brooke is chatting with Jesse. She's leaning against her locker with her arms crossed under her boobs to make them look bigger.

Chloe grabs my arm. "What's up with that?"

"Nothing." I focus on getting my shorts and T-shirt out of my locker.

"That is *so* not nothing."

I head for the bathroom and lock myself in a stall so no one can see the tears forming in my eyes. Em and Chloe follow me and stand outside the stall. "What does Brooke think she's doing?" Chloe asks.

"It's complicated," I say from inside the stall.

"It's not complicated. She's a man stealer," Em spits out.

"Complicated how?" Chloe asks.

"I can't tell you now."

"Can we talk after school?" Em asks.

I open the stall and daub my eyelashes to stop the flow of mascara. "That would be good." Chloe and Em both hug me, and we stand in the bathroom ignoring other girls until the bell rings. I stay in the bathroom until I'm sure Brooke and Jesse are gone. I'm late for phys ed and have to run laps, but I don't care.

Chloe and Em are waiting for me by the lockers after school.

"We feel bad. We've been so busy, we didn't even know something was going on with Brooke," Chloe says.

"Man stealer," Em whispers.

Chloe elbows Em in the ribs. "Wanna come over?" she says to me.

I nod, and we head out into the drizzling afternoon. At Chloe's house we settle in the TV room with popcorn and cranberry juice. I feel like doing something mindless—watching TV or even playing video games—but Chloe and Em want the dirt.

"So, what happened?"

"Well, Brooke says she's in love with Jesse."

"But he's yours," Em wails. "He even writes you poetry."

"We're just friends."

Em stuffs her face with popcorn. "Could you please stop saying that? We're writing a musical about you two."

"You are?"

"Yeah, want to hear?"

Em and Chloe look at each other and then sing, "Oh he's a goy and she's a Jew and they don't know what to do. Teen lo-o-o-ve."

"You're kidding, right?"

Chloe flops back on the couch. "Okay, we just made that up after school, but c'mon, what happened?"

I sigh. "I guess you didn't see, but when we were at the park the other night, the guys, including Jesse, were dressed up as Nazis. And I totally freaked out at him about it."

Chloe sits up. "Wow, that's really bad."

Em crinkles her brow. "Nazis? As in the guys who killed all the Jews?"

"And lots of other people too. Anyway, I guess Brooke can laugh it off, but I can't. And she's 'deeply in love' with him."

"Did you say 'deeply'?" Chloe asks.

"Yep."

"I think I'm going to barf." Chloe holds her hand over her mouth.

"You could write it into your musical instead."

"Ooh." Em rubs her hands together. "Now we've got conflict. A Smoker girl is trying to break up the young cross-cultural lovers. What will Lauren do?"

"I don't think anything rhymes with cross-cultural," Chloe says.

"How about interracial?" Em suggests.

Chloe cocks her head to the side. "They're not technically interracial or even mixed ethnicities."

"Guys, please."

"Sorry," Em says.

"Anyway, I want to—I don't know—disappear for a while. I can't watch them at school. And I sit between them in biology. But I can't be there."

"That's so crazy," Chloe says.

"What would you do?" I ask.

Chloe and Em look at each for a moment and then Em says, "Well, I would pray about it."

My eyes open wider. "Look, guys, I don't want to be rude, but I don't think that's my thing."

"No, you should try it," Chloe says. Both of them are looking at me earnestly.

I take a deep breath. "C'mon, it's not like if I pray for Brooke not to like Jesse she'll stop. The world doesn't work that way."

"No," Chloe says, "but it might make you feel better."

"Yeah, I don't think so."

We sit quietly for a moment, eating the last of the popcorn. "I'm going to pray for you tomorrow at Bible study anyway," Em says. "If that's okay."

"Yeah, sure."

"Me too," Chloe says.

"You go to Bible study too?"

"Yep. Every Tuesday morning at seven thirty."

"Wow. That's early. What exactly do you do there?"

"Well, we usually read a section of the Bible and talk about it, and then we have a short prayer session and maybe a talk from Cathy."

"Who's Cathy?"

"She's our group leader."

"Hey, you should come tomorrow morning." Em grips my hand. "It's at my house, and my mom's making pancakes for everyone."

"I'd feel awkward."

"We'll have a special prayer for you, except we won't say your name or anything."

"Well…"

"Think of it as a learning experience."

"I'll think about it."

I leave soon after to walk home. It's pouring now, and the rain runs off my jacket, soaking my jeans. I've never thought much about prayer. To me, it's the chanting you have to do at Hebrew school while your teacher makes sure you're not daydreaming. And if I did pray, what would I ask for? For Jesse not to have dressed up as a Nazi? No, I'd pray not to be Jewish; then I wouldn't care what Jesse wore.

When I get home, my parents are pacing the kitchen. "What's going on?" I say. "Don't you guys work anymore?"

Mom taps her long burgundy fingernails on the counter. "No one can find your brother."

"Oh."

Dad leans on the counter, brow furrowed. "Do you have any idea where he might be?"

I shake my head. "Did he go to school?"

"I dropped him off this morning," Mom says, "but he left at lunch and no one knows where he is."

I listen to the rain drumming on the skylight. "Well, I'm sure he'll show up when's he ready." I quickly head down to the basement, in case Mom and Dad start fighting. They used to argue a lot when Zach was still at Hebrew school and hiding all the time. Zach would hide if his phys ed class was too loud or if his schedule changed unexpectedly. He hated fire and earthquake drills. Even a class party would throw him out of whack. Every time Zach hid or, worse, ran away from school, I'd end up sitting with him or looking for him until Mom left work to get him. I'd hate how Zach looked when I'd find him hiding in the equipment closet with his hands over his ears, or under the librarian's desk with his eyes closed. I'd always want to hug him, but I knew that that would be too much contact for him when he was feeling overwhelmed. Instead I'd sit quietly beside him until he was ready to come out of hiding. Zach's been much happier since he transferred to a special private school a couple of years ago.

In the basement, I sit on the stool at the workbench. I've decided to make a star lantern. It's got a lot of straight lines, so it shouldn't be too hard. I've made some sketches, and now I'm trying to cut the wood, but the saw keeps slipping. Maybe I'll figure out how to suspend a candle in a cheese grater instead. I saw a few people with lanterns like that last summer, and they looked pretty cool too, but not as cool as the dragons, cupcakes and aliens.

I think the real reason I'm having so much trouble making a lantern is that when I close my eyes and imagine myself at the festival next summer, I'm not walking around with a lantern, I'm spinning a burning hula hoop around my waist, around my arms. I'm surrounded by flames, yet not burning.

This will definitely not happen. I'm not the performing type. Not even with an unlit hula hoop.

I pick up the saw to try again, and then I hear a tapping sound. At first I think it's the furnace, or maybe the water heater, but then I hear it again, coming from the laundry room. I think of mice and yank my feet up onto the stool, but it's not really a scurrying sound. I have a moment of panic, and then it occurs to me: Zach. "Who's there?" No response. "Hey, Zach," I whisper, "is that you?"

I get a cough in response.

"Cough twice if it's really you."

Zach coughs twice. I breathe a sigh of relief and stick my head into the laundry room. "Where are you?" The closet door slides open a bit, and I see two eyes peeking out from behind the ski suits.

"What are you doing?"

"Nothing." Zach's eyes blink in the darkness. I hear his toes tapping on the linoleum.

"Oh. Wanna come out?"

"No, thanks."

I cross my arms and tap my toes back at him. Then Zach asks me, "What are you doing down here?"

"Trying to make something."

"What?"

"Just this art project."

Zach steps out of the closet, his hair full of static. "Can I see?"

"Well, sure."

He follows me to the workbench and stares at the mess of wood and sawdust.

"I'm trying to make a lantern."

"A what?"

"A lantern—you know, something you put a candle in. It's made out of tissue paper, wire and wood."

"Oh. So what's the problem?"

I hold up the two uneven pieces of wood. "I can't saw straight."

"Did you use a vise grip?"

"What's that?"

"It's this thing that holds the wood steady."

"I don't think Dad has one. How do you know about that?"

"Shop class. I actually like shop class. Did you know the lathe in the shop at school can turn a block of wood into a baseball bat in less than five minutes?"

"I didn't know that."

"Can I make a lantern too?"

"Sure."

Zach looks at my drawing. "I think you need a better design first. Like, draw it out and do the measurements."

"Oh, good idea."

Zach pulls some paper across the table and hands me a piece. He starts sketching a biplane.

"So, why were you hiding?" I ask.

Zach doesn't say anything, so I focus on my drawing. Then, just when I think he's not going to answer, he says, "Bar mitzvah lessons."

"Not going well?"

He shakes his head.

"What's the problem?"

"I don't want to do it."

"The practicing? I'm sure you'd learn it superquick, if you wanted to."

"I don't want to."

"Oh? Why's that?"

"'Cause then you have to do it in front of all those people."

"You mean the guests."

"Yep. Do you know how many people were at your bat mitzvah?"

"How many?"

"Two hundred and thirty-seven."

"You counted?"

"Yep. I can also tell you how many lights are in the sanctuary."

"I bet you can. So what are you going to do?"

"Hide. Refuse to go anywhere."

"Refusing to eat works well."

"Really?"

"Worked for me."

"What if I did all three?"

"That might work. Plan your snacks in advance."

"Oh, okay." Zack puts down his pencil and points to my picture. "Lauren?"

"Yeah?"

"Can I draw that for you?"

"Sure."

"Your design kinda sucks."

"Thanks a lot."

Zack shrugs, sketches out the star and then adds the measurements. "Why a star?"

"I don't know. I just like them."

"That's weird."

"I wouldn't talk."

Zack pretends to look offended.

I stay in the basement until I get hungry, and then I go upstairs and let my parents know I've found Zach.

"I thought you looked down there," Mom says to Dad.

"I did."

"Well, obviously not very well."

"Please don't start," he says.

"Hey, before you guys get going, do you want to know why Zach is hiding in the basement?"

"Let me guess." Mom runs her hands through her hair, tugging on the blond strands. "He didn't want to go to his bar mitzvah lesson?"

"You got it."

Mom rubs her temples. "I was worried this would happen."

Dad sighs. "Maybe we should find him a different tutor."

I lift my hand as if I'm at school. "I don't think Rabbi Birenbaum is the problem. Zach doesn't want to have a bar mitzvah because he hates being the center of attention."

Mom sits down at the counter and holds her head in her hands. "But it's a special occasion, and I really want him to have the same opportunity as the other kids."

I hold up my hands in defeat. "Is there anything for dinner?"

"Don't look at me," Mom says. "I've spent all afternoon looking for Zach."

Dad sighs and opens the freezer. "How about hamburgers?"

"Sounds good," I say.

Dad defrosts the burgers and grills them on the barbecue on the back deck, under a golf umbrella, while I cut up lettuce and tomato. Zach comes upstairs once he realizes it's too late to go to his bar mitzvah lesson. He's all smiles as he eats voraciously, smearing mayonnaise across his face. Although Zach is a better eater than he used to be, he still avoids brightly colored foods like ketchup and mustard.

"Are you going to hide next week too?" Dad asks wearily.

Zach shrugs and shows Dad his biplane drawing. I can see it's a big effort for Dad to show any interest.

After dinner I spend a few minutes working on my history essay. Mr. Whiteman approved my thesis and outline ages ago, but I haven't opened the books I checked out of the library yet. I've done some research on the word *genocide*, since that's what most websites call the massacres in Armenia. Basically, it means the intentional killing of a whole group of people because of race or religion. I've heard about genocide in Africa, in places like Darfur and Rwanda, but when I do a Google search, lots of places I didn't know about come up, including Cambodia and Indonesia and Bosnia. It freaks me out, reading about all that killing. I'm finding more and more holocausts all the time.

I lean back in my chair. It isn't only the killing that's getting me. At every Holocaust memorial and ceremony I've been to, Jews have said, *Forgive but never forget.* The other thing they've said is, *Never again.*

And yet it is still happening, over and over again. How many millions of people have died as a result of genocide since the Holocaust? It makes me feel sick to my stomach. When Jews said *Never again*, did they only mean to them?

I find something else that is disturbing. When I key in *Jews + genocide* in Google, not only do I get articles about atrocities committed against Jews, I also get articles about atrocities committed *by* Jews. One of the articles is about the Israeli army oppressing Palestinians. I don't know much about the Israeli-Palestinian conflict, but just reading this makes me feel crazy. Is this the end result of the Holocaust? Jews got a homeland in Israel and the Palestinians lost theirs? I'm not sure, but it makes my head ache to think about it.

I put away the books on Armenia without opening them.

Before I get into bed, I check my phone.

Alexis has written: Did u tell?

I don't reply. Next there's a message from Brooke. U still mad?

I text back No.

Brooke writes back U pissed?

Yes.

Don't be.

OK.

U lying?

Maybe.

My place aft school?

Busy.

I wait to see if she texts back, but the phone is silent. I get my biology textbook out of my bag and try to read the assigned chapters, but then my phone beeps again. It's Em. Pancakes and prayer @ 7 am. U in?

Not sure.

C'mon, it'll be interesting.

Yay God?

Yep, yay God.

I think about it for a minute. Then I write, OK, curious. Will b there.

Yay! Go in side door. Don't knock. Peeps sleeping.

I type back g-nite and put the phone down.

This is weird. I'm going to Bible study, to pray about Jesse. No, I'm going to observe a cultural experience. It'll be interesting.

I set my alarm for 6:00 AM, turn off my light and roll over. I close my eyes and try to breathe deeply, but I'm not sleepy, so I look on my night table for something to read. I've finished *The Color Purple*. Then I remember that the Mengele book is still under my bed. I'd meant to put it back on Dad's desk, but I forgot. I get it, put it back, then pick it up again. I shouldn't, but I want to read to the end of the book so I can learn how Mengele was eventually tried and punished. Surely he must have died a horrible death after all the misery he caused. Instead I learn that Mengele escaped through Italy and went on to South America. Anger rises like heat on my skin when I read how the killer lived out the rest of his life without any punishment while the twins who survived had all kinds of physical and psychological problems. How could they not? Almost all Mengele's survivors were the only people in their families alive at the end of the war.

I slam the book shut and shove it under the bed again after I read that Mengele believed he was doing real scientific research. Science, my ass. I clench my teeth and feel tension building in my neck. And the guys at school, they thought it was funny to pretend to be Nazis. Calm down, I tell myself. It's just ignorance. If they knew about Mengele, they wouldn't have done it.

Maybe Dad is right. Maybe the world still needs more Holocaust education. I flop over in bed. This is so complicated. I'm sick of hearing about the Holocaust, yet there are still people who don't know about it or make light of it. Where's the balance? Should I tell someone about the armbands and hope the guys get some sensitivity training? Is the Holocaust so big and terrible that absolutely everyone has to know about it?

I close my eyes and try to think about playing basketball with Jesse, or being at the lantern festival. It doesn't work. I can't stop thinking about the book, and the more I think about Mengele cutting people up, the more I feel panic rising in me, like bile seeping up into my throat. My fists tighten, and I press my toes against the footboard of my bed. The book feels like a hot coal burning under my bed. I try to do the five senses exercise: I can see the damn book; I can hear the voices of the boys laughing in the park; I can taste anxiety boiling in my throat as I imagine killing Mengele. How would I do it? Would I let him starve, or would I shoot him? Maybe I'd gas and burn him. I sit bolt upright and throw off the covers. The Nazis are turning me into a killer. I can't distract myself—not with the book in my room. I have to get it out of here.

I creep quietly down the stairs to Dad's office. Dad is at his desk, leaning back in his chair, reading. I think about casually walking in and putting the book on the shelf, but he's sure to ask me what I'm doing. I could wait until tomorrow, but I want that book away from me now. Just looking at it makes me feel panicky. What kind of idiot was I to think I could read it? I stand there in the hallway outside his office and suddenly realize that I want the book out of the house altogether. At the back door, I pull on my raincoat and boots and slip into the yard. It's a cold, clear night, and the stars are pinpricks of light in the sky. I inhale a few times and watch my breath cloud into the air. What if I dumped the book in someone's garbage? If I head out the back lane, though, I'll trigger the motion-sensor light by the back gate. Instead I slip into the darkened garage and shove the book on a shelf under the sun umbrella. There, I think. Rot in the garage, killer.

Nine

My alarm rings before it's even light outside, and I peel myself out of bed. Em lives a few blocks away in an ancient mansion with beautiful woodwork and enormous fireplaces. Her house is so big and formal, I feel weird letting myself in the side door.

Fortunately, the Bible group isn't meeting in the living room—which reminds me of a funeral parlor from a movie, with lots of high-back sofas and long creepy drapes—but in the blue-and-white TV room on the second floor. When I arrive, lots of girls are already there. I recognize kids from school, some I didn't even know were Christians. Everyone speaks in whispers, although somewhere in the house I can hear kitchen cupboards opening and water running.

I sit next to Em and she introduces me to Cathy, a woman who looks younger than our moms but older than a college student. She has long blond hair in a braid down her back and is wearing a loose plaid shirt.

"Lauren's just observing today," Em says.

"Great." Cathy smiles. "Feel free to join in."

Cathy calls the group to attention and asks them to turn to Mark 12. I decide to sit back from the group, on the window seat. I watch the girls flip through their Bibles and listen to Em read several verses, ending with, "Thou shalt love thy neighbor as thyself. There is none other commandment greater than these."

Em pauses and Cathy turns to the group. "So what should we make of this?"

There's a moment of silence, and then a girl I don't know says, "Well, I think it means we should be good friends."

I sit up a little straighter as the girls discuss what it means to be a good friend. I've never heard the Bible talked about as actually relevant to our lives. At Hebrew school, we talked about Jewish history or what the different rabbis said or how to fulfill Jewish commandments.

After the discussion, each girl shares her prayers for the day. Chloe is first. "I pray to understand math and get along better with my mom. And for all my friends to be happy." She looks over at me.

The next girl says, "I pray for my sister to stop taking my stuff." Everyone laughs. "And for Claire to be okay with her parents' divorce." Everyone looks at a girl named Claire, and she tries to smile.

Another girl I don't know says, "I pray for my grand-mother to recover from her operation, and I'm thankful for Em's mom's pancakes." More laughter.

Claire waves her hand in front of her mouth when it's her turn, so Cathy says, "We all pray for Claire to be strong and to be helped by her friends through this diffi-cult time. And we hope she knows Jesus is her friend."

Claire says, "Thank you."

I knit my brow. Jesus? How is Jesus your friend if he died for your sins? Then Em says, "I pray for all my friends to make the right decisions and feel peaceful." She looks at me across the room.

The other girls pray for help at school or with personal problems. Cathy says, "I pray for Jesus to show us all how to live and that all your hopes and dreams will come true. Amen."

The girls all say, "Amen," and then they hold hands and smile as they send a "prayer squeeze" around the circle.

Then we go downstairs to the dining room, where Em's mom is standing at the table with a huge platter of pancakes. Em passes me a plate. "See, isn't Bible study amazing?"

I nod. I'm not sure what to say. It's all so…personal.

"Is Jewish prayer like that?" Em asks.

"Um, not really." But I can't explain why. Em's mom comes over to ask her something, and I'm saved from having to explain. Despite seven years of Hebrew school, I've never really prayed. I've recited the Hebrew prayers millions of times, and I know what most of them mean, but they aren't my words or wishes. Jewish prayer is ritualized and thought out in advance. You say thanks for various things and praise God a zillion times, then you say a prayer for the sinners and for good health and praise God another zillion times—he's a king, he's a lord and a whole bunch of other male images—and then it's finally over. I can't think of a single time in all my years of Hebrew school when anyone said, *Pray your own prayer.* Making a wish when I blow out candles on my birthday cake is the closest I've ever come. How depressing. Eight years of Hebrew school has actually deprived me of the chance to pray. If I were going to write a list of reasons why being Jewish sucks, this would be near the top.

I wander away from the chatting girls to find the bathroom. On my way back, I spot what must be the library. Unlike Dad's cluttered, book-filled mess with its Ikea furniture, this office is regal. Built-in bookshelves and a fireplace surround a huge desk. I sit on the floor near the entrance and listen to the girls' chatter. Someone is discussing a math test, and I hear snippets of talk about a soccer game.

Jewish youth group is so not like this. At the one event I attended before I declared myself not Jewish, we played broomball and ate pizza. The girls worried about what their hair looked like, and the guys goofed off on the ice.

I tuck my knees up to my chest and rest my cheek on my folded arms. Tears come to my eyes, and I blink them back. I'm envious, not because they believe in God or because Jesus is their friend, but because they have each other.

I pull a book off a shelf near me to distract myself from self-pity and realize it's an old book of maps of China. I stand up and look at some of the other titles. There are Bibles, lots of books on Christian missionaries, and then a whole wall of books on China. I wish Dad's office was full of these kinds of books.

The girls start leaving, calling their thanks to Em and her mom and Cathy. Then I hear Chloe calling me. I step out of the library and into the hall.

"I'm here," I say.

"Oh, good." Chloe and Em already have their coats on. "Cathy's going to drive us to school. Are you ready to go?"

"Yeah, sure."

"Are you okay?" Em asks.

"Yeah. Fine. Thanks for inviting me. It was cool."

"You could come again, if you like."

"The lone Jew at the Christian prayer group?"

"Well, you could say your own prayers, if you like."

I feel tears well up. "I must be really tired."

Em and Chloe both hug me. "We'll keep praying for you even if you don't come," Chloe says.

I hug her tighter.

In biology class I sit on the aisle and concentrate on the video Mr. Saunders shows. I can tell Jesse glances at me several times, but I keep my eyes forward. At lunch I sit with Chloe and Em and listen to them study for an English-lit test.

Down the hall, Brooke, Chantal and Kelly surround Jesse. He looks like he's enjoying himself, surrounded by three sets of cleavage. I notice Brooke has started wearing low-cut tops. Jesse doesn't look over at me once. I sigh.

By the end of the day, I'm exhausted from my late night with Mengele and my early-morning Bible study. I go home after school and get into bed and fall asleep. When I wake up an hour later, it's dark outside, and I snuggle under the covers and play games on my phone. I can always do my English reading later. Then I hear Mom calling me for dinner. I'm about to put my phone down when I notice a voice message. From Jesse. I feel my pulse start to race. Shut up, stupid heart. But it doesn't. I play the message.

"You must think I'm the biggest jerk ever, and insensitive and racist. And I'm not. Look, we were drunk and it seemed like a good idea at the time, and no one thought, What's the Jewish girl going to think? And we should have. So let's go running and I'll apologize all the way. And when we get back, you can beat the crap out of me at basketball. I'll even let you win. Just kidding."

Which emotion should I experience first? How about ecstasy? He called me. He wants to play basketball with me *and* go running. And he said he was wrong. That's enough, isn't it? I actually have to stop and clutch at my chest to make sure my heart doesn't jump out of it. Can you die of excitement? Can you die from your heart actually beating too fast and...I don't know, overexerting yourself? Probably not, if you're a healthy teenager, or people would die from sex all the time, and that only happens to old men.

And then there's the angst. What about Brooke? Am I supposed to say, *Oops, he's not a total Nazi, just kinda dumb and I've forgiven him, so get lost?*

"Lauren, dinner is on the table," Dad calls.

"Coming."

I let my parents and Zach chat through dinner and focus on eating Mom's delicious salmon. I don't know how she does it, but she makes it with this maple-ginger glaze that's awesome. I eat two helpings, and Mom smiles.

When I'm clearing the table, Dad hands me an envelope. I look at the return address and hand it back to him. It's from the youth group again.

Dad raises one eyebrow. "Hey, you promised to at least think about going."

I sigh and rip open the letter. What is it this time? A symposium on Jewish song, a debate on intermarriage? No, it's a pamphlet for March of the Living, a Holocaust tour for teenagers that reenacts the walk Holocaust victims took from the Auschwitz concentration camp to the Birkenau camp.

"Why would they send me this?" I throw up my hands.

"That tour ends with a couple of weeks in Israel. Wouldn't that be fun?" Mom says hopefully.

"You're kidding, right?" I look at Mom. "Please tell me you think this is funny."

Mom puts down her scrub brush and dries her hands on a dishtowel. "I don't think it's funny at all. I think it's educational."

I drop the pamphlet onto the counter and rub my forehead. "Wait, let me get this right. I've already told you I'm sick of the Holocaust and think it's way overdone, but you want me to experience more Holocaust, in Poland, and then get on a plane and go to Israel?"

Mom loads the dishwasher with the dirty plates. "Shayna Shuster says Rebecca went last year and loved it."

"Rebecca Shuster is an idiot."

Mom gives me a pained look. "I know you haven't been very interested in doing anything Jewish, but this might help you reconnect with your Jewish roots."

I slap my hands against my thighs. "UNBELIEVABLE."

"What's the problem?" Mom asks.

"You really don't get it?"

"No, it seems like a nice idea. You might even meet a nice Jewish guy."

I can't decide whether to laugh or cry. I start hiccupping instead. "Absolutely no effing way would I go on that trip."

"Hey, language," Dad says.

"Are you guys out of your minds?"

Mom sighs. "What's the problem?" she asks again.

"I know I'm not supposed to tell you guys you're stupid or anything, but COME ON!"

"Enough with the theatrics. State your case." Dad crosses his arms against his chest.

"Okay, so you take a bunch of teenagers to Poland, and you stuff them with ideas of how Jews were hated for centuries and then finally exterminated in gas chambers. And then, when they're filled with misery and have begun to see themselves as victims, you fly them to Israel and tell them they're free, that they have their own homeland. Then they support Israel no matter what it does, even if it means killing Palestinians. You're turning kids into Holocaustarians."

"Did you say Holocaustarians?" Dad asks.

"Yes, I just made it up. There are people who are Christians or Buddhists or vegetarians or whatever, and then there are people who are Holocaustarians. And not just any holocaust, but the one with the capital *H*."

"Let's not go down that road again."

"I can't believe you were stupid enough to show me this pamphlet!"

"It just came in the mail…" Dad says.

I stomp out of the kitchen and go up to my room. I'm so angry, I feel like slamming my door a hundred times. Instead I pull on my running clothes and take the stairs back down three at a time. Mom comes into the front hall as I'm pulling on my mittens.

"Where are you going?"

"For a run."

"At night? I don't think so."

"Watch me." I slam the door.

Outside it's damp, and the wind whips the last leaves off the trees and sends them scurrying down the street. I sprint down the block until I'm panting and have to walk. I nudge the wet leaves with my running shoes. I've forgotten to bring an elastic, and my hair blows around my face. It's too cool to keep walking, so I start a slow jog.

Why do people have to keep reminding me I'm Jewish? And worse, why do they keep using the Holocaust to do it? I don't get it. If Jewish organizations want to teach kids about their Jewish heritage in a positive way, they should send them to Spain, so we can see the sights of the Golden Age when Jews and Muslims lived together in harmony. I learned about that in grade-eight history.

I start to calm down as I jog through the streets. I like looking into people's houses when their lights are on. Inside, people are eating dinner or watching TV. No one is getting killed or massacred or planning on killing someone. At least, I hope not. A few cars pass, and I see someone walking a dog. Then I hear footsteps coming up behind me, running footsteps. I tense and look over my shoulder. Another runner, a guy, is coming down the street—fast. Too fast. I'm about to cross the road when I hear someone call, "Hey, Lauren." I turn and realize it's Jesse. "Wait up," he calls.

I stop and wait until he catches up.

"What are you doing out here?" I blurt.

Jesse's panting. "I saw you go running by and…well, I thought I'd go for a run too."

I can't help smiling. "Oh."

Jesse starts jogging beside me. "How far are we going?"

"I'm not sure. It might be a long run."

"All right, I like a challenge." He lifts his hand to high-five me. I think about ignoring it; then I see his face, sort of eager, and I notice he has beautiful, perfectly sculpted eyebrows, as if he's had them professionally shaped. A little tingle travels down my legs, and I reach over and smack his hand.

I let Jesse set the pace and the route. I'm too nervous to think of anything to say. Usually I turn around at Sixteenth Avenue, but Jesse keeps heading north. I did say I was going on a long run. Rain starts to fall, not a downpour but more of a gentle mist, and I try to rescue my hair by pulling up my hood. After a while I relax a little. Jesse looks cute in his track pants, his hair hanging down in his eyes. Every block or so, he pushes his hair behind his ear, and it stays there for about half a block and then falls down again.

The closer we get to the beach, the windier it gets. By the time we reach the road next to the beach, the wind has whipped strands of my hair loose from my hood and sent them flying around my head. I can't imagine what my hair will look like by the time we get back.

"How far are we going?" I finally say.

"Oh." Jesse looks at me. "I don't know."

"We should turn around." My parents will kill me if they find out I was down by the beach at night.

"If we go a little farther west, it's not such a steep hill home."

We jog along the waterfront, the puddles lit up by passing headlights. When we get to a grassy park, Jesse grabs my hand. "Hey, wanna go down to the beach?"

I don't want to, but Jesse's holding my hand, so I squeeze his hand yes and let him lead me down a steep flight of stairs to a gravel path above the rocky shore.

The wind roars around us, damp and unruly, swirling off the water. It's dark on the path, but across the harbor, downtown shimmers, and beyond that the lights on Grouse Mountain twinkle.

Jesse laughs into the wind. "Isn't this amazing?" I shiver and nod, smiling wildly. I feel like I could lean into the wind and it would support me, and I wouldn't go careening into the rocks.

"Okay," Jesse says, and he points his thumb to the stairs. We sprint up the steps and stand in the lee of a huge tree. I hunch over, trying to catch my breath as I wipe my eyes. Jesse stretches his quads. I try not to stare at him as I run my hands through my hair. I know my cheeks must be bright from the run.

"We should get going."

"Run too far for ya?"

"My parents are going to kill me for being gone so long in the dark."

"They notice that kind of thing?"

"Sure. Don't yours?"

"No, not so much."

"It's 'cause you're a guy."

Jesse shrugs. "I think they got used to not having me around. You know, being away at school and all."

"Oh. You happy to be back?"

"Yep." He smiles at me, and I flex my legs nervously.

My sweat starts to chill. "We should get going."

"Wait a second." Jesse grabs both of my hands. "You never texted me back."

"Oh." I look up into his face. "I guess I didn't know what to say."

Jesse squeezes my hands. "Well, how about you say, 'I accept your apology.'"

"Um, okay. Yeah." I'm so nervous, I can't think. The wind is pushing my hair into my face, and I'm worried I might smell from the run. Jesse steps closer to me and I let him, even though I know I shouldn't. I should pull away and say, *Race you to the intersection.* Instead I let Jesse pull me close enough that I can put my head on his shoulder. I'm so close, I can hear him breathing. My own nervous breath is coming so fast, I'm sure I sound like I'm having an asthma attack. Then Jesse lets go of my hands and his arms wrap around me, his hands smoothing the back of my running jacket. I inhale noisily and feel my cheeks flush. I stay absolutely still, holding my breath, my face resting on his shoulder. I'm supposed to do something with my arms. Letting them dangle is not an option. I take a deep breath and wrap my arms around his waist. I'd like to squeeze him tightly and prove to myself that this is for real, that Jesse is actually hugging me. I don't dare. I'm so nervous, I'm not even enjoying the hug. How pissed off will Brooke be?

Then I feel Jesse starting to pull away a little and I think, Okay, this is going to end, and we'll jog home, and maybe we'll forget about this. Maybe we'll call it "that time we once hugged by a tree near the beach." Omigod, that sounds so romantic. Then Jesse leans down, his lips moving warm and wet on mine. I can taste the salt from his sweat. I stop thinking about Brooke or anything but Jesse's delicious lips. I'm so out of breath I'm sure Jesse will notice. He'll say, "Yanofsky, you breathe like a truck."

But he doesn't. He nuzzles my ear and says, "I've wanted to do that for a long time."

I don't say anything. I can't say anything. But I pull away and let him see the smile spreading across my face. It's the kind of smile that's so big it feels like my face might crack. I grab Jesse's hand and pull him toward the intersection and then back up the street toward home. I flap my arms, pretending to be a bird or a plane.

It's a long run back, but when I feel tired, I look at Jesse, and the smile he gives me makes me think I could fly all the way home.

We run down the back lane behind our houses and I say goodbye at my garage. "Wait," Jesse says, but I don't want anyone to see us, so I just wave and slip through the back gate.

As soon as I'm out of sight, I throw myself against the garage door. Omigod. I can't believe it. He wants to kiss me. He did kiss me. I do a small jig and trigger the motion-sensor light. Mom opens the back door.

"Lauren, is that you?"

"Yep, it's me."

"We were worried. Where have you been?"

"On a really long run."

Mom sighs. "It's not safe for a girl alone."

"Yeah yeah. Whatever."

"We'll take you to the gym, or you can use the tread-mill here."

"Yeah, okay." I want to be alone, so I slip past her and run up to the shower.

I strip off my clothes, stand under the hot water and do a little happy dance. I want to tell Brooke, but we're not talking. How can I not share this with her? I want to tell everyone. But I won't. I'll keep this secret to myself. I wrap my arms around myself in the shower. Jesse wants to kiss me. He did kiss me. I do another happy dance.

Ten

The next day, I'm so nervous that I don't leave for school until I'm almost late for biology. How can I sit between Brooke and Jesse for ninety minutes? When I arrive, Jesse grins at me and kicks my leg under the stool. I ignore him and pray he stops. I glance at Brooke, but she's staring straight ahead. Luckily, Mr. Saunders is introducing a new unit on mammals, and there's no lab. Soon we'll start dissecting a fetal pig, which sounds disgusting.

Jesse catches up with me on the way to English. "Hey, what's the hurry?"

"I have to go to the bathroom before class starts." I'm speed-walking down the hall, dodging grade eights.

He jogs to keep up with me. "You mad at me again?" He grabs my hand and makes me stop.

"No, just nervous." I pull my hand away and look around. Brooke has gone ahead to her math class.

He steps on my toe. "What are you nervous about?"

"I don't want people looking at us," I whisper. "I…"

"It's a secret?"

"It's—I don't know—private, I guess. You won't say anything, will you?"

Jesse cocks his head. "I can't write *Jesse thinks Lauren is a babe* on the bathroom wall?"

"No."

"How about *Jesse kissed Lauren by the beach?*"

"No!"

"How about—?"

I step on his toe. "How about nothing?"

Jesse sighs. "Girls are weird."

I shrug, and we walk to English together.

While I'm waiting for class to start, I check my phone. Alexis has texted me. Did u tell?

I sigh. Jesse kissed me at the beach, I write back.

OMG! U still have to tell.

I put my phone away.

After English I grab my lunch from my locker and walk to the auditorium to watch the *Grease* rehearsal. I can't possibly make it through lunch with Jesse. I'm sure everyone, especially Brooke, will know about us by the way he looks at me. So instead, even though I want more than anything to sit and hold Jesse's hand, I munch my bagel with cream cheese, tomato and sprouts and listen to the *Grease* cast sing. Em's voice is better than it was last year. I realize she must hold back when she sings with us, because here in the auditorium, her voice fills the space. She's almost convincing as Rizzo, although she still looks too prim.

When the bell rings for third period, I go to my locker to grab my clothes for phys ed. Brooke and Jesse are sitting on the floor, listening to Brooke's phone, each of them with one earbud in. Jesse sees me and gets up. "Hey, where were you?"

"I, um, was watching *Grease* rehearsal."

"Oh." He nods. "Run later?" He raises his eyebrows.

I feel like everyone is watching—or at least, Chloe, Em and Brooke are. "Maybe, if it's not raining." I want to stay and look at him leaning against my locker with that sexy smile on his face, but the second bell rings. "I have to go now. See you later."

Brooke glares at me and starts walking beside me to the gym. "What was that about?"

"Nothing. He was just being nice."

Brooke sighs. "He is really nice, isn't he?"

"Yep."

"Did you hear Tyler's having a party at his house Friday night? It's his birthday."

I nod. It's the first time Brooke and I have spoken all week. "I was thinking of asking Jesse if he'll go with me."

"Oh." I stop in the hall. "Did you ask him yet?"

"No, not yet. What do you think? Should I call him or text him or message him on Facebook?"

My stomach twists. "Why would I care?"

"Could you please get over yourself?"

"Not likely," I say under my breath as I stalk off.

Mom makes a delicious chicken stir-fry with broccoli and snow peas for dinner. She's in a good mood because Zach has agreed to study with a college student for his bar mitzvah. I can't quite read what Zach is thinking now, but I'm sure he has some alternate plan.

After dinner I load the dishwasher and Dad scrubs out pots and pans while Mom pores over an invitation catalog at the table. Zach sits next to her, building with Lego. Mom asks Zach, "Now, do you like the navy and gold, or the navy and silver?" Zach just shrugs.

"Why don't you email people?" I say. "It's way more environmentally friendly."

"Tacky." Mom doesn't look up.

Dad gives me a warning look. "Don't rain on your mother's organizational parade," he whispers.

Mom is in full bar mitzvah planning mode. She has a baking day at the temple lined up, a booking at the

Richmond Country Club for the party, and caterers to interview for the Saturday lunch. "I think I like the silver." She marks the page with a sticky note and closes the catalog.

Zach ignores her and pulls more Lego out of a plastic bin. His starts tapping his toes on the floor.

"So, what do you think?" Mom asks Dad. "Deejay or band?"

"What about a jazz quartet?"

"Could they play a horah?"

"Probably not."

"Then no. Ooh, what about a klezmer band?" she says. Dad makes a face.

"You don't like klezmer?"

He makes another face.

Mom turns back to Zach. "How about you? What do you think?"

Zach focuses on attaching wheels to a Lego car. "I'm not going to the party."

"What are you talking about?"

"I hate those parties. They make you play games and dance with girls."

"Hey," Dad says, "girls are okay."

Mom grips the invitation catalog. "What do you mean you're not going to the party?"

"I never agreed to that."

"What are you talking about?"

"I said I would study my Torah portion with the cool guy if you bought me the space-station Lego set, but I never agreed to anything else."

"Zach, I'm about to spend a lot of money to book the country club."

"Well, I'm thinking about being out of town that weekend."

"Where are you going?" I ask.

"I thought Palm Springs might be nice that time of year, but I might have trouble at the border since I'm a minor, so I might have to settle for Whistler or Kelowna or Surrey."

Mom sighs. "Zach, this is unreal."

I can't help smiling. "She's not going to give up, is she?" I whisper to Dad.

He pokes me in the ribs. "Don't antagonize your mother."

I finish the dishes and go to the computer. Mom's still badgering Zach, but he's shut down and refuses to answer her at all. You'd think she'd have figured out by now that badgering doesn't work with Zach.

Then the doorbell rings. I hear Dad open the door and say, "Hey, Jesse, what's up?"

I sit bolt upright in the chair. Omigod, he's at my house? This is crazy.

I hear Jesse say, "Hi, Dr. Yanofsky. I'm here to go running with Lauren."

I stand up as Dad calls me. Jesse's already dressed in a pair of running tights, a red toque and a blue jacket with a hood. "You up for a run?" he asks.

"Um, sure." Couldn't he call first?

"I'll wait for you, if you like." He winks at me and then turns to Dad. "I saw Lauren out by herself last night, doing wind sprints, and I thought it was pretty dark to be running alone."

"That's exactly what we thought. You two should start a running club."

I roll my eyes and head upstairs to change. I hear Dad say, "So, nice to be back in the neighborhood?"

"Yes, sir, glad to be back."

I can't believe he's here, that he wants to see me again. I look in the mirror. I'm not curvy like Brooke or sexy like Chloe. I do have nice skin, but I still don't get it. Why does he like me? I'm actually stiff from running last night, and part of me feels like saying, *Forget it, I can't take this much excitement.* I sit on the floor and pull on a pair of socks anyway. Maybe I can just tell him the truth. Which is what? Brooke is in love with him? I can't say that. Maybe I should call Brooke and tell her the truth. That I'm in love with Jesse and he's here in my house? I can't do that either.

So I pull on some running pants, grab a long-sleeved top and a fleece jacket and braid my hair, pulling it tightly into an elastic. I say goodbye to Dad, and then Jesse and I head out the front door.

The night is crisp and cool, with stars visible overhead and a half-moon glimmering. As we start running down the street, Jesse grabs my hand. I look at him, smile and then pull away.

"Hey, let's go this way." Jesse guides me down the steep slope past the railway tracks to the grassy hill of the park. He stops under the trees, away from the road, and pulls me toward him. He kisses me, a little more roughly than last night, his hands sliding down my back, pressing my pelvis against him. I can feel that he's hard through the thin layer of his running pants.

I pull away. "Hey, I thought we were running."

"I thought we could warm up first." Jesse kisses my neck. "You smell good." His hands work their way under my running jacket and skim along the top of my pants.

I suck in my breath and pull away again. "Look, sorry, but…"

Jesse rubs his hands over his face. "No, I'm sorry." He strokes my cheek. "It's just…you're so—"

I cut him off before he says something embarrassing. "Look, let's just go for a run."

Jesse sighs and reluctantly drops his hands. "Yeah, a run. That's a good idea."

We jog up the tracks to Forty-first Avenue, through Kerrisdale and then back. We don't say anything the whole time. Crap, now he's going to think I'm frigid, that I'm not worth his time. Where is the damn line, and how do you straddle it?

When we get back to our street, I let Jesse lead me down the lane, let him press me up against the garage. I can say goodbye and slip into the backyard anytime if I want to, end this if I need to. Jesse keeps his hands on my back the whole time. And yet, as my lips cling to his, I realize I'd like him to squeeze me tightly again. He smooths my hair instead. When we break apart, my cheeks are flushed. "I should go," I say, "but I don't want to."

Jesse nudges me with his shoulder. "See you tomorrow at school, where I won't talk to you."

"I heard Tyler's having a party tomorrow night," I blurt out.

"I'll be there. You?"

"Yeah, me too."

He smiles. "See you," he says; then he jogs down the lane.

Eleven

On Friday night, Mom, Dad, Zach and I are invited to the Shusters' for dinner. Not only do I have to sit through dinner with Rebecca, but her dad is on call and so dinner doesn't start until really late. Jesse texts at eight thirty to ask if I want a ride to the party, but dinner is still dragging on and I have to say no.

By the time I leave the Shusters', Chloe and Em have already walked to the party and it's now too cold to bike, so I take the bus to Tyler's house and go in the open basement door.

The large hedge in front of Tyler's house makes it perfect for a party. From the street, no one can see the kids or the lights. Because it's Tyler's birthday, only certain people are invited: the Perfects, the basketball team, the Smokers, some of the cast of *Grease*. I've heard of other parties where everyone texts their friends and people end up trashing the place, but this doesn't happen with my friends; it's kind of an unspoken rule.

In the basement, Tyler, Mike, Justin and some other basketball guys are hunched over a coffee table playing quarters, a drinking game where you have to bounce a coin into a shot glass. Jesse isn't with them, and I feel my toes curl up in my shoes. Maybe he's not coming. Chloe and Em are sitting in front of a huge TV with some other members of the *Grease* cast, drinking cans of pop and discussing whether Chloe should cut her hair into bangs or if it will make her look too young. "You'll lose your romantic look," Em says.

I sit down on the saggy faux-leather sofa and pretend to be interested in Chloe's hair. Mac burps loudly and the boys cheer. Chloe and Em roll their eyes.

Em moans, "How am I ever going to wear hot pants onstage? They make my thighs look horrible."

"Black," Chloe says. "Tell Mr. Romano that hot pink is not your color, even with the wig, and you need black. I have some you can wear."

"You think it'll help?"

"Immensely." Chloe flaps her hand. "Hey, do you think Nick—the guy who plays Danny—do you think he shaves his chest?"

I don't pay attention to Em's response. The guys are laughing about the time Justin got wasted at the beach, the time Mac barfed in his mom's planter. I'm too nervous about seeing Jesse to be in a party mood. Besides, drinking until you're sick is gross. After a few minutes, I go upstairs to look for Jesse.

I'm about to step onto the back porch when Brooke comes out of the bathroom. She's wearing a really short skirt and a tight low-cut top and carrying a beer.

"Hey, you're here!" Brooke leans toward me. "I came with Jesse," she slurs.

"Super. Text or Facebook?"

Brooke ignores my sarcastic tone. "I called him." She sounds triumphant.

"That's just fabulous." I start to push past her, but Brooke grabs my hand. "I asked him for a ride, and he said okay." She giggles drunkenly.

"Like I said, fabulous."

"He said he'd drive me home too." Brooke digs her fingers so tightly into my arm, it feels like a claw. Then she turns toward the back door. "Everyone's outside. Coming?"

I shake my head no and watch Brooke carefully make her way down the back steps to the patio, where Chantal and Kelly are sitting. Brooke sits on a lounge chair next to some guy and throws her arms around him. I step onto the back porch, pulling on my jacket. Brooke must be freezing, I think. The voice in my head sounds like Mom's, and I shudder. How does that happen? Then I realize Brooke has her arms around Jesse.

Just as I'm about to walk down the stairs, Tyler, Mike and some other guys push past me and run down the stairs, yelling. They're carrying squirt guns and wearing black toques and the swastika armbands. I stand frozen to the spot, as if one of them had slapped me. The guys run around the yard and then out the gate to the back lane. I can hear them whooping by the garage, calling the other guys to join them. I watch to see if Jesse will join them. He doesn't. All he does is pull away from Brooke as he watches the guys go past. Then he sees me on the stairs. I'm not sure how to read his expression. He's smiling, but it's an awkward half smile, and I'm not sure if it's because he's sitting with Brooke or because the guys are playing the Nazi game again.

He starts to stand up, but then the guys with their Nazi armbands burst back into the yard, yelling drunkenly and jumping over lawn furniture on their way back out to the lane. Kelly, Chantal and Brooke laugh as the guys knock over a chair and spill a beer. Justin and some other guys from inside join them. I step back into the kitchen to get away from it all and press myself against the wall. I can't believe they're all just sitting there while the guys are playing Nazi again. Yet I can hear Kelly describing some campground while Mike organizes the guys in the back lane. I should stand up and say, *Hey that's offensive*, or rip their armbands off. Wouldn't they find that funny? I should go back downstairs or just leave—anything to be away from the boys with their armbands, from Brooke drooling over Jesse.

Back in the basement, Chloe and Em and some other girls are talking about a shade of nail polish called Aphrodite's Nightie. Some other kids are smoking a joint and listening to Pink Floyd's *Dark Side of the Moon*. I try sitting with Chloe and Em, but I'm too restless. The guys are pretending to be killers in the back lane, Brooke's hitting on Jesse and he's just sitting there, and here I am, listening to a conversation about nail polish. I slip into the bathroom on the main floor and sit on the edge of the tub for a few minutes, looking at my nails. I don't want to be at this party anymore. I leave without saying goodbye to anyone and go out the front door. Down the street, two people are getting into a blue Honda. I take a few steps forward and squint. It's Jesse and Brooke. I watch Brooke laugh and teeter drunkenly. Jesse is holding her arm, helping her into the car. Brooke bumps her head on the roof, and they both laugh. Then Jesse does his lanky, sexy walk to the driver's side, shaking his hair out of his eyes.

I stand, stunned, watching them pull away. Does Jesse have his arm around the back of Brooke's seat now? Is he squeezing her shoulder the way he squeezed mine? Was Jesse using me, or am I missing something here? I shake my head, trying to clear it. I'm cold, and I feel like I need to sit down, so I walk toward the bus stop. As I step into the street, I see something white in the gutter. At first I think it's a bus transfer or a beer cup, but then I look again and realize it's one of the swastika armbands. I crouch down and look at it. I should grind it into the pavement or rip it into shreds. Instead I brush off the dirt and shove it in the pocket of my jeans.

Back at home, I sit on the damp concrete floor of the garage, delaying going inside. The lights are still on in the house, and I don't feel like talking to my parents. Also, my hair smells like smoke. I gently bang my head against the garage wall.

No matter what I do, the Holocaust keeps finding me, like a bad smell I can't get rid of. I even sense it in the garage because of the Mengele book. I wish I'd found somewhere better to hide it than in here. Whenever I think about that book, I feel hate welling in me. Hate for Mengele, for the Nazis and for the world that let Mengele do those things. I even hate the authors for writing the book.

The automatic garage light goes out, leaving me in the dark, and I wrap my arms around myself, shivering. I used to be scared of the dark; now I'm scared of becoming the kind of person who is filled with hate. It's more than sixty years since the Holocaust and here I am, still worked up. And I'm not even Jewish anymore. At least, I'm trying not to be. I never did come up with a good "de-conversion" ceremony, and I've never told anyone about my non-religious status. I should have taken out an ad in *The Independent*, the local Jewish paper: Susan and David Yanofsky regret to announce that their daughter, Lauren Michelle Yanofsky, is no longer a Jew. Donations for counseling gratefully accepted.

I should have tried harder to come up with a ritual or ceremony for becoming un-Jewish. A symbolic burning would have been great. I could have torched my bat mitzvah certificate. Becoming a bat mitzvah is supposed to mean you are responsible for your own religious life. If I burned that piece of paper, would I feel more free? I sit upright, humming with energy.

I close the garage door, moving across the lawn and into the house quickly and quietly. Mercifully, the lights are out now, except for the night-lights illuminating the stairs. I want to get into the house and leave again without anyone noticing. I'm sprinting up the stairs with my jacket still on when Mom calls, "Lauren?" from her bedroom.

I freeze halfway up the stairs. "Yes?"

Mom sticks her head out the door. "I wanted to make sure you got in safely."

"Yeah, I'm fine."

"Was that you in the garage?"

"Yes."

"What were you doing out there?"

Oh…" I pause. "Just thinking."

Mom gives me a weird look. "I'm glad you got in early." She blows me a kiss. "Good night."

"Night."

I stay still until there's no noise from my parents' room, then dash up to my room and shuffle through the contents of my desk drawer. My bat mitzvah certificate is still tied with a baby-pink ribbon. I race back down the stairs, grab a box of matches from above the stove and slip out the back door. The sensor lights flick on, and I stop and look up at my parents' bedroom. Their room stays dark, so I continue out the back gate to the lane. I lean against the garage a moment to catch my breath. I'm sweating, even though it's cold and damp outside. I tuck the certificate under my arm and scrape a match against the sandpaper on the match-box. A deep sigh moves through me as the match bursts into flame. I hold up my bat mitzvah certificate and bring the match to it. The cheap paper burns quickly. I drop it when it gets too hot to hold and stamp out the flames. It's over way too fast.

I wander down the lane, shivering a little. I wish I was on a beach with a raging bonfire, one hot enough to warm my hands or cook baked potatoes. If I had a big enough fire, I could raze all my father's horrible books. Or just one book, the Mengele book lurking in the garage. That would be enough. I shudder. The Nazis burned books to try to destroy Jewish culture. I'm acting like them. It's their hate getting to me. I shrug off this idea. I want to burn the Mengele book so I'll never have to read it again.

I pause, mulling over the idea. And then I spring into action, rummaging in the garage behind the sun umbrella. The book will make a bigger fire, one that'll last longer. Back in the lane, I tuck the book under my arm and light a second match. It's drizzling now, and the match hesitates before catching flame. Then I hold the book by the spine, pages spread, and light it on fire. My breath is ragged now, my pulse racing as if I had just sprinted up a hill. The pages twist and bend in the flames, and then the whole book starts to flicker. It's like a flaming flower, so beautiful I wish I could photograph it. I feel the flames grow hot against my palm before the book is even half scorched, and I know I should drop it on the pavement and move it down the lane with a stick so it doesn't leave a mark on the pavement, but it looks so stunning, I don't want to let go. I feel the heat on my palm, excruciating yet also exciting. I suck in my breath a moment longer and then drop the book. I grab a stick and push the ball of flame down the lane, like I'm playing field hockey. I want to take a slap shot, but I resist and gently bat the book across the asphalt. My next lantern could be a hockey stick with a flaming puck. When the flames die down, I stamp them into ashes. The scorch mark is small and won't show on the pockmarked lane.

I skip down the lane, still holding the stick in my hands. I made a ball of flames, and it was unbelievably gorgeous. Then I chuck away the stick and start to sprint. When I stop to catch my breath, I feel a burning sensation on my palm. In the backyard I examine my hand under the sensor light. I instantly become aware of pain when I see the burn on my palm. Oh fuck. How the hell am I going to explain this? Still, I'm kind of pleased. This is my mark of conversion. I imagine un-converting other people from religious backgrounds as a way of creating world peace. We could all bear scars on our palms as marks of our journey.

In the house, I thrust my hand under cold running water and force myself to wash it with soap. It hurts so badly, I have to stamp my foot so I don't scream. I take a few deep breaths and then quickly wrap my hand in gauze. I realize I'm sweating from the pain, so I treat myself to two extra-strength painkillers.

I lie on my bed, too keyed up to sleep. I batted a burning book down the lane. I got rid of the Mengele book. Holy shit, I think, I even burned my bat mitzvah certificate. I want to get up and tell someone, but who? Everyone would think I was crazy. My hand starts to ache really badly. How am I going to play basketball or even hold a pen? What if it gets infected? How will I explain the burn? An accident? I roll over, and something pokes my hip. I pull the armband out of my pocket. I should have burned it too. I slide it into my night-table drawer to get it out of sight, change into my pajamas and lie in bed listening to my noisy pulse. Finally, the drugs kick in, my head becomes groggy, and I fall asleep.

My throbbing hand wakes me up the next morning. Shit, I think, infected already. It's raining steadily outside, making the light coming through my window a flat gray.

I lie in bed and think about the Mengele book, reduced to ashes. All the information from that copy is now either part of the atmosphere or ground into the asphalt in the back lane. Except for the part that has eaten away my hand and is still burning away in my mind. I shake my head, but even that movement makes my hand hurt. I take two more painkillers and put on an old sweatshirt over my pajamas. The stretched-out sleeves dangle over my hands.

Dad is in the kitchen, drinking coffee and reading a brochure for a Holocaust Studies convention. Mom's probably driving Zach to swimming lessons.

"Good morning." Dad looks up from his reading. "How about pancakes?"

I yawn and lean on the counter. "Sure."

Dad puts down the brochure, and I pick it up and start reading. "Hey, Dad, can you please tell the Holocaust people to hold the conference in Hawaii next year?"

"Hmm, not so many Holocaust historians live in Hawaii."

"Yes, but the Holocaustarians might like the beach."

"Right." Dad sighs. "Can you get the pan for me?"

When I reach down to open the drawer, the bandage on my hand peeks out from my sleeve.

"What happened to your hand?"

"Nothing."

"Let me see that."

"It's nothing."

Dad grabs my hand and looks at the gauze. "Honey, what happened?"

"It got a little burned."

"Burned? How did you get burned?" Dad's eyebrows shoot up his forehead.

"Oh, we had a fire at Em's in the fireplace, and a log fell out and I grabbed it."

"How bad is it?"

"It's nothing, really."

He gives me a skeptical look. "That's an awfully big bandage for nothing. I think we should get your mom to look at it."

"She's a nutritionist, not a nurse. And she's not even here." I get up to leave.

"Lauren."

"Yes."

"Unwrap your hand."

"It's nothing."

"Lauren, now." Dad has a look in his eyes I haven't seen in a long time, not since I told Zach to fuck off in front of the rabbi during my bat mitzvah photographs.

"Um, okay." I lean on the island and peel off the bandage. I was too freaked out to even look at the burn this morning.

Dad lets out a long whistle. "Get your health card and get in the car."

"What about the pancakes?"

"Pancakes? Are you nuts?"

"I'm hungry."

Dad's voice gets louder. "Lauren, go get dressed, then get in the car."

We drive to emergency at Children's Hospital and sit in the waiting room, not talking to each other. I try to read *The Tempest* for school, but I can't concentrate. Dad focuses on his Blackberry, texting Mom the highlights of our wait.

After an hour I say to Dad, "It's not like they're going to do anything about it."

"What, you're a burn specialist all of a sudden?"

"So I'll have a little scar."

"Lauren, you're missing the palm of your hand." He says this way too loudly, and people stare at me.

I start to cry. "It was an accident."

He puts his arm around me and squeezes my shoulder. "I know. I'm just worried. How are you going to dribble with your hand in a bandage?"

This makes me cry harder. My hand is killing me now, absolutely throbbing. "You don't have to wait, if you don't want to," I say through my tears.

"Of course I'm going to wait."

I keep expecting him to ask me more about the accident. But he doesn't. I feel guilty. I mean, I burned a book. I burned *his* book. I imagine telling him the truth: my friend went out with the guy I'm in love with while his friends were playing Nazi, and so I came home and burned a Holocaust book in the back lane. He'd take me over to the psych ward. Maybe I should be there. I start to feel panicky, so I focus on my breathing.

When it's finally my turn, the doctor who examines my hand looks like Whoopi Goldberg. She doesn't ask me what happened, just cleans the wound, which hurts like hell, and prescribes Tylenol 3.

"Denny's for pancakes?" Dad asks as we leave the hospital.

"No, thanks." I want to curl up in bed, maybe listen to some music.

Mom is waiting for us when we get back. I'm expecting an inquisition, but instead she hands me a glass of water and pulls back the covers for me. "We'll talk later," she says.

I swallow the painkillers, pull the covers over my head and cry. I'm not sure if it's because of the pain or because my parents are being so impossibly nice or because I burned a book. Mostly, I think it's because I can't get that image of Brooke and Jesse out of my head.

Twelve

Zach has made nine plane lanterns, each in a different design and color, since he found me trying to make my star. My favorites are a red biplane, a yellow bomber and a helicopter painted bright turquoise. Each plane has a spot for a candle in the cockpit. Zach's lined them up as if the workbench is a busy runway. Next to the planes are more drawings, each with Zach's carefully drawn ruler lines. The wood Zach cut for my star is still neatly stacked on top of the design he drew for me, but I know I won't bother to make it. The picture I drew looks boring next to Zach's elegant planes, and I crumple the paper and shove it in the garbage bin under the bench. Maybe I'll take Zach and his lanterns to the lantern festival next summer, although he hates crowds.

I sigh and listen to the hum of the furnace and the other quiet noises of the house on a Monday afternoon. It's pouring outside and windy: I can hear the rain blowing against the basement windows, funneling through the gutters. I rest my head on the worktable, still woozy from the painkillers, my burned palm pulsing like sonar. I almost fall asleep, but then my neck gets sore, so I go back to bed. When I open my bedside drawer for more Tylenol, I see the Nazi armband. I take it out and look at it. I should have burned it with the Mengele book and my bat mitzvah certificate. But I didn't, and now it's here, like a gory bit of evidence. I should send it to the Holocaust museum Dad volunteers at, further evidence of ongoing anti-Semitism in the modern world. Jews, take cover: the Holocaust lives on, even if just in the minds of ignorant teenage boys. Alexis still thinks I should tell the school or my parents. She'd probably call the Anti-Defamation League headquarters in New York and make it international news: *Teenage Boys Play Nazi.* But that's not it, that's not it at all. This isn't about hating Jews; it's about boys and their guns and their stupid games. Like Jesse said, it's just a bunch of guys in the park.

And it's about Jesse, who isn't a Nazi, isn't my boyfriend, either, and possibly is not even a friend. He hasn't texted me all weekend. I'm just part of a game of guys, guns and interchangeable, disposable girls. I roll over in bed and punch my pillow into a new shape. Nothing is sacred to them—not history, not relationships.

I finger the armband—the staples, the thick white paper, the swastika drawn with a ruler and filled in with black markers. It makes me think of the Mengele book, even though that book is ashes in the lane. I twirl the armband around my finger, hold it up to the light, bend the edges until the paper becomes soft. What should I do with it?

1. Throw it out and forget about it (except I won't).
2. Let it sit in my drawer and drive me crazy (except I'm already nuts).
3. Turn it in, like Alexis says (except everyone will freak out, the boys will get in lots of trouble and great— the Holocaust will be front-page news again).
4. Shove it in between the books in my father's office amid the millions of words about Nazis, death and torture. Let it be another bit of tragedy, another bit of hate. No one will notice it there.

I get out of bed and go down to Dad's office. I look at the books and shudder, feeling surrounded by war, hate, hunger, disease and death. One day when I have my own place, I'll have a library, or at least a bookshelf, with nothing on it but books on peace and novels about women.

I hear the click of the front door and Mom's heels on the tile foyer, followed by the squeak of Zach's sneakers. I quickly shove the armband between two books on the Warsaw Ghetto and go into the front hall.

I hear Mom say, "Then the Lego goes." Mom looks supermad; her lips are pressed so tightly together that they form a thin, hard line. She's taking her coat off so fast, I think she might rip the buttons off.

Zach stamps his foot. "That's so unfair."

"Look, we had a deal and you've broken it. Study with the tutor, learn *all* the parts for your bar mitzvah, or suffer the consequences."

"You said I had to learn the Torah portion. No one said anything about leading the whole service. You keep changing the rules."

Mom puts her hands on her hips. "Do I need to spell out every aspect of what we expect you to do? All the kids lead the service; you know that."

Zach glares at Mom. "I'm not doing it."

"Then the Lego goes."

"Then forget the whole thing," Zach mutters.

"Fine. You can kiss your video games goodbye too."

Zach sits down on the staircase. "That's so incredibly mean. I *need* my games."

"Well, maybe you should start thinking about making some compromises," Mom snaps.

There's a long pause. Zach scrunches up his forehead and fiddles with the zipper on his hoodie. Then, very softly, he says, "No. Compliance is not an option."

"What's that?" Mom says.

Zach stands up. "Where are the sleeping bags?"

"What do you need a sleeping bag for?"

"I'll be spending the duration of my hunger strike in the garage. So I'll need a sleeping bag to keep warm. When you're ready to abandon plans for my stupid bar mitzvah, I'll be happy to eat again."

Zach goes down to the basement, presumably to find a sleeping bag.

Mom throws up her hands. "This is ridiculous."

Mom makes grilled-cheese sandwiches for dinner to entice Zach to the table, but he has already gone out to the garage.

"Just leave him," Dad says. "I'm sure he's got a stash of crackers or pretzels. If he doesn't, he'll be in soon enough."

"And in the meantime"—Mom crosses her arms— "what am I supposed to do? Miss a day of work?" She looks at me. "Am I going to have two kids at home tomorrow?"

I swallow a bite of sandwich. "I'm going back to school."

"Feeling better?" Mom says.

I nod.

"Good. That's one kid." She hands me a mug of tomato soup.

Dad helps himself to another sandwich. "Zach's twelve. He can stay at home by himself. He'll get bored eventually. Then he'll eat and go back to school."

Mom taps her fingernails on the table. "We're totally caving in to him."

Dad sighs. "Let's wait it out. If he's still out there tomorrow, then we'll reconsider."

"I wish Zach didn't see his bar mitzvah as such an ordeal." Mom gestures toward me. "Lauren loved her bat mitzvah."

"Yes," I say. "The gifts and party were a great finale to my Jewish education."

Dad gives me a warning look and gets up to refill his drink. Mom looks like she might spit at me.

"Look," I say, "I can tell you exactly why Zach's freaking out. He doesn't want to perform like a trained monkey in front of all of your friends."

"This isn't about performing," Mom hisses. "It's about becoming a Jewish adult. It's a rite of passage."

I can't help snickering. "Fine, let him become a Jewish adult, just not in front of the entire community. It's too scary for him."

Mom puts down her soup spoon. "But the community needs to celebrate all our kids, especially Zach."

"I don't think Zach sees it that way."

Mom glares at me across the table. I glare back.

In the morning, I spend at least five minutes trying to straighten my hair using my left hand. In the end, I ask Mom to help me, and because she's my mom, she doesn't say a word about me being rude last night. She just takes the straightener and quietly runs it through my hair, combing with her fingers. She even flips the ends under the way I like.

Mom and I don't say much at breakfast. She sips her coffee and tries to avoid looking out at the garage. Zach refused to come inside last night. I'm not sure why he has to stage a hunger strike in the unheated garage. Additional risk due to exposure? You never know with Zach.

I nibble my toast and try not to think about sitting through biology between Brooke and Jesse. I'll sit on the aisle, pop a painkiller to dull my general awareness and let them do their lab together. It'll suck, but it won't kill me, right? I mean, there are worse things in the world, like getting struck by lightning or drowning.

I'm putting on my rain boots by the front door when I get a text from Jesse.

Walk with me?

What the hell? No thanks, I text.

U still sick?

I hold my phone in my hand, not sure what to write back. Does he think he can pretend he didn't go to the party with Brooke, or that I don't care? I feel anger creeping up my spine like mercury rising up a thermometer. The idiot probably thinks the world revolves around him, and maybe it usually does. I resist the urge to throw my phone through the window. Instead I write Y u care? Then I stick the phone in my bag.

I feel hot in my jacket, my blood pounding in my head. Why aren't people nicer? I jam the tip of my umbrella into my boot with my good hand. Ugh. I'm so sick of guys who think they can do anything without consequences. Pretend to be a Nazi and then apologize. No big deal. Kiss a girl and forget about her. Enough. Crap happens when you do shitty stuff—or at least it should.

Instead of walking out the front door, I find myself marching to Dad's office and my hand going up to the shelf and pulling the armband from its hiding space. Then I write the names of all the Nazi boys on the inside of the armband. *Mike, Tyler, Mac, Justin, Jesse.* I add the words *pretended to be Nazis* after their names. I'm using my right hand, even though the burn hurts like hell and I can feel my scab breaking open, oozing pus into the gauze. I shove the armband into my pocket and let my anger fuel me out the door without saying goodbye to Mom. I run down the street, boots clomping on the pavement, and then across the field. I don't stop until I get to school, where I lean up against the wall, breathing hard and sweating inside my rain jacket. I should throw the armband out, just rip it up and stick it in the garbage. My phone buzzes again, but I ignore it.

I walk into the school—it's early still and not many kids are around—and head toward the guidance offices. I slip in and pull a university calendar off a shelf, pretend to be interested in it. I hear two of the counselors talking in the hall and then see them walk toward the office. Ms. Chung, one of the counselors, has left the door to her office open. I look around, pull the armband from my pocket, drop it on her desk and then dart back to the hall.

I trot up the stairs to biology class, even though the bell won't ring for another thirty minutes and Mr. Saunders isn't there yet. I sink to the floor, still wearing my boots and jacket. My hand is throbbing now, and a wet stain has leaked through the bandage. My phone buzzes again, and I sigh and check my messages. Jesse, the idiot, is still texting me: miss u.

I write Y u care?, and his response is miss u.

My breath catches in my throat. I imagine Jesse with his phone, his hair hanging in his eyes, his tongue out the way it is when he's concentrating on taking a shot in basketball. Wait a second. Who cares if he misses me? He's still an idiot. But I miss him too, even if that makes me an idiot as well. And a loser. And a doormat. I'd let him walk all over me; I know I would. All weekend, when my hand hurt so bad I wanted to scream, I kept thinking about kissing him, about the way it felt when he wrapped his arms around me. Even when I thought about him leaving the party with Brooke, I still missed him.

I put my phone back in my bag. I don't know what to text back. Maybe *miss u 2 even tho u r an a-hole?*

Brooke and Chantal slip into class just as the bell rings. Brooke doesn't even look at me, and I don't turn her way. Jesse arrives after the bell rings and receives a glare from Mr. Saunders. Jesse sits at the end of the row, beside Chantal, and doesn't look at either Brooke or me. When biology is over, I try to leave class quickly, but Jesse is right beside me.

"I came by your house this morning, to see if you wanted to walk together."

"I left early today." I stare straight ahead.

"Hey, what happened to your hand?"

"Nothing."

He grabs my arm. "Why are you so mad at me?"

I stop. "You have to ask?"

"Look, if this is about the party, I can explain."

"Oh." I start walking again, too embarrassed to look at him.

"What happened to your hand?" he asks again.

"It got burned."

"How?"

"I can't tell you now."

We arrive at English class. "Let's talk at lunch," Jesse says. He gives me his old cocky smile, and I feel myself melt a little.

"Not then. Maybe after school."

"Okay, I'll wait for you." He smiles again, but it's a small smile, kind of nervous. He looks almost shy.

We go into English class and I take out my phone and look at the miss u message again. I'm a puddle on the floor.

I'm a rag doll he can arrange anyway he wants. I'm a chocolate melting in Jesse's pocket.

Then I think about the armband in Ms. Chung's office with the names on it—with Jesse's name on it. I squeeze both of my hands into fists, and the edge of my burn rips a little more. I bite my lip as pain ricochets across my palm.

At lunchtime I sit with Chloe and Em, trying to copy notes from yesterday's classes. Jesse sits down the hall, listening to music on his phone, with his head buried in a math textbook. Since it's not only raining but windy and cold as well, Chantal, Kelly and Brooke are inside too, looking bored. Brooke doesn't glance my way, but I notice she isn't looking at Jesse either. I can't concentrate on the notes because of what Jesse might say later and because of the armband sitting on Ms. Chung's desk. Maybe she'll curl her lips in disdain and sweep the armband into the recycling bin. Maybe she'll think it's a bad joke, not worth following up. I tip my head from side to side, trying to unlock the kink in my shoulders. My palm pulsates like a kick drum.

Then I see Ms. Chung walking toward us down the hall with Mr. Petrovic, the principal. Their eyes fix on Mike, Tyler and Justin, playing cards in front of their lockers. They stop at the end of the hall, faces grim, arms crossed in front of their chests. I clench my fists again, almost willing the pain to spread through my hand—anything to relieve the tension building in my gut. Shit, I should never have turned

in the armband. A major witch hunt is about to happen.
And it's my fault. I take a deep breath, swallow hard, but
it doesn't help. I know this feeling; panic starts like a sour
taste in my mouth. I should do my relaxation exercises.
Instead I get up and take my phone into the bathroom, lean
my head against the wall of a locked stall and text Alexis.

I did what u said, I write.

Alexis texts back immediately. Armband?

Yes.

That was the right thing to do.

It's going to b ugly.

Always is.

I want to live somewhere beautiful.

Don't we all?

The bell rings and I text: Don't tell anyone.

Lips sealed. U r going to b ok.

Hope so.

After school Jesse silently waits for me to pull on my
boots and jacket. I can barely look at him, not even when
he holds my bag open so I can slip in my books. "Does
that hurt?" He points to my hand.

"Yep."

"You going to tell me how it happened?"

"Maybe."

Jesse smiles. "You're in a weird mood."

"Yep," I repeat. I'm feeling almost giddy as we walk down the hall, because nothing matters anymore. I've already lost Brooke, and I've kissed a boy who probably doesn't love me and then turned him in for playing at being a Nazi, which means he'll hate me if he finds out it was me. What else is there to lose?

Jesse says, "Come over to my place?"

I shiver and nod.

Outside it's blowing rain so hard, I don't bother opening my umbrella; it'll only flip inside out. It's too windy to talk, so we trudge silently across the field, heads down against the wet wind. When we get to Jesse's house, we peel off our wet layers in the mudroom off the kitchen.

Jesse lives in a mock Tudor house with green shutters that sits atop a small hill of a front yard. Inside there's lots of wood trim, built-in shelves and stained-glass windows. Even though it's pretty big, Jesse's house has a comfortable, lived-in feeling. Nothing's too fancy, and all the rooms have leaded-glass doors, so you can have privacy if you want it. Not like my house.

Jesse makes us hot chocolate and then leads me through the living room to a small den at the side of the house. At first the room is dim, but Jesse turns on a lamp and pulls the curtains against the rain-splattered windows. Then he flops onto a corduroy couch across from a small tiled fire-place and holds out his hand to me. "You look cold."

I ignore his hand and sit in a wingback chair across from the couch. Jesse points to my bandaged hand. "So, what happened?"

I look down at my hand. "I burned it."

"How?"

"Fireplace."

"Ouch." He moves closer to me, lifts my burned hand to his face, kisses my wrist. I let my eyes close for a second, then pull away.

"Wait."

"What for?"

"You can't just kiss me."

"You weren't complaining last week."

I scoot back in the chair and pull my knees into my chest. "What about Brooke?"

Jesse groans and drops his head into his hands. "Can we forget about her?"

It's so quiet I can hear my watch tick. Jesse rubs his forehead.

"I saw you leave the party together," I whisper.

"Yeah, that was a mistake." He looks up at me and smooths his damp hair off his forehead.

"What's that supposed to mean?"

"It means it was a dumb thing to do." We're talking softly, almost as if this conversation isn't happening.

"I—I don't understand."

Jesse sighs and lifts his head. "Look, she's your friend and I don't want to bad-mouth her."

"So what were you doing?"

Jesse sighs. "Okay, she calls and asks for a ride to the party. And I think, she's your friend—right?—and we talk at school and all, so sure, I can drive her. I think maybe you'll be coming with her too."

I hug my knees tighter to my chest as he continues.

"Brooke says Chantal and Kelly need a ride too, but when I get to her house, it's only her. So fine, we get to the party and we're hanging out in the backyard and everything's cool. Then she gets pretty drunk, and she asks for a ride home, which is weird, 'cause it's early, but I figure maybe she isn't feeling so great. So I ask the other girls if they want to go, but they say no. I look for you, to see if you want a ride, but you've disappeared. And so I drive her home."

"And that's it?"

"Well..." Jesse reddens. "She tried to—you know, come on to me, but I was like, *Whoa, no thank you.* I mean, she's your friend."

"I'm not sure we're friends anymore."

"Really?"

I nod.

"So that's it. I'm not interested in Brooke or any other Smoker chick. They wear too much eye crap. I'm interested in you. So stop being mad at me, okay?" Jesse takes my hand and pulls me onto the couch next to him, kissing my wrist again. I feel my pulse start to race. He looks up at me. "Okay?"

"Um, okay," I whisper. Jesse squeezes my arm with both his hands, leans in to kiss my neck. I want to say, *Stop a minute, let me think this all through*, but Jesse's kissing my throat now, making little shivers scurry through me. I'm imagining Jesse fighting off Brooke because he likes me, not her. I feel myself smiling under the little ticklish kisses he's laying on my lips. "You like that?" he says. I murmur yes and kiss him back. Jesse pulls me onto his lap and I wrap my arms around him. We could go for another run, and kiss by the beach again, and maybe even hold hands at school. I could come to his house and do this again. I run my hands through his hair. Jesse's kisses are moving away from my throat and down the V-neck of my sweater. He doesn't like Brooke, and he's not a Nazi. Then I remember the armband. I stop playing with his hair and open my eyes. I slowly pull away from him. He smiles at me and picks up my hand. "So what really happened to your hand?"

"It got burned," I say.

"You shouldn't play with fire." His hands slide up my thighs.

"I have to go." Suddenly, I can't hold all the thoughts in my head.

Jesse flops back on the couch. "Girls always do that, just when it gets exciting."

I stand up and swallow back a nervous smile. "I need to get home and deal with my bandage, and Zach's doing this hunger strike."

Jesse crinkles his forehead. "For, like, world peace or something?"

"No, it's more complicated." I straighten my sweater. "I'll have to explain another time." I start backing up.

"Wait, I want to ask you something." Jesse stands up and put his hands around my waist. "Can we stop with the not talking at school? It's too weird."

"Oh, okay."

"And you could, like, eat lunch with me too."

"Um, sure."

"Tomorrow?"

"Okay, tomorrow." I duck my head as my cheeks heat up.

"Wait, don't leave yet." Jesse pulls me closer and kisses me. It lasts forever, and I don't want it to stop. "Are you sure you need to leave?" he whispers.

"I'm sure." I sound unconvincing, but I manage to turn and walk out of the room.

Jesse and I walk to school together the next morning, holding hands under a stark fall sky. An early frost makes the grass crunch under our feet as we walk across the park. I let go of his hand as we walk into school, and he rolls his eyes at me.

"What?" I say.

"Chicken." He squawks and flaps his arms. I smile weakly, but I'm so nervous I can't think straight.

I walk to biology with Jesse, and we sit next to each other on our stools. When Brooke and Chantal come in, I see Brooke glance at us, then turn away. Jesse squeezes my good hand under the desk. I take a few deep breaths and try to think about Zach, still in the garage in his sleeping bag. He refused to eat or come in yesterday, and Mom and Dad had a huge fight about it. While they were yelling, I sneaked Zach a cheese sandwich.

Mr. Saunders starts class and I think, I can do this. I can do the rest of my life—Brooke, Jesse, the armbands— and then the phone in the class rings, and Mr. Saunders answers. He listens, nods and then hangs up. "Tyler Muller, Mac Thompson and Jesse Summers, you're wanted in the office," he says.

The class collectively says, "Ooh," and my stomach plummets. Jesse smiles self-consciously as he packs up his binder and textbook. Everyone is staring at him, Tyler and Mac. After they leave, Mr. Saunders continues lecturing, but I'm not listening anymore.

Jesse isn't in English class. Mr. Willoughby has us act out a scene from *The Tempest*, and luckily he doesn't ask me to read. Right before the period ends, he reads out a note. "Oh yes. Tomorrow, period three and four classes are not being held as regularly scheduled." Someone lets out a cheer. Mr. Willoughby puts up his hand. "Instead, you are to go to the auditorium for a special guest lecture by Professor Mark Yanofsky. Dr. Yanofsky is an acclaimed Holocaust historian and a dynamic speaker. It is hoped that all students will benefit from his lecture and accompanying film." He puts the paper down and takes off his reading glasses. "I understand there was some sort of incident, something about Nazis in the park." He winces with disgust. "Please take a notice with you on your way out." The bell rings and Mr. Willoughby says, "Off you go."

Students stream around me, but I can't get out of my chair. This is worse than I could possibly have imagined. Not only do all the grade eleven and twelve classes have to attend a lecture on the Holocaust, but it's being given by my father. My father! This is the final proof that there is no God. God couldn't be this cruel to an innocent girl.

Mr. Willoughby stops me on the way out. "Lauren, are you related to Dr. Yanofsky?"

"Um, yeah, he's my dad."

"Interesting. I've heard him speak before, at my church. He is an excellent speaker."

"Oh, thanks."

At my locker, I find Jesse sitting on the floor, knees bent, head resting on his arms. My fingernails dig into my good hand as I clench it into a fist. "What's going on?" I slide down the locker and sit next to him on the floor.

Jesse turns his head sideways to look at me. "Aw, someone ratted us out about the Nazi game. Mr. Petrovic had one of the armbands, and someone had written all our names on it."

I should act surprised. And shocked. Horrified? That would be overdoing it. "Wow, that's crazy," I manage to say.

"Yeah, we got an in-school suspension and we had to write letters to our parents explaining what we did. My parents are going to kill me."

"Oh." I swallow.

"Shit." Jesse pounds my locker. "They'll probably start talking about boarding school again."

I catch Chloe looking at us, but she looks away when our eyes meet. "Did you hate it there?" I say quietly. I draw my knees up to my chest so I'm sitting like Jesse. Neither of us pays attention to the kids moving down the hall for lunch.

"Aw, it was all right, it's just not the same as here."

I nod and relax a little now that we're not talking about the armbands. Then I see Justin, Tyler and Mac coming down the hall, holding notices about the assembly.

"This is totally stupid," Mac says, crumpling up the paper. He bats it down the hall.

"Yeah," Tyler says. "They should thank us for making fun of Nazis."

Mac elbows Tyler. "Hey Muller, you Germans should sit in the front row."

"Hey, shut up. Your grandparents are lederhosen too."

Mac grabs Tyler's ballcap and throws it down the hall like a Frisbee. "No way, loser, they're Polish."

Justin looks over at me. "Hey, Lauren, is this your dad or something?" He holds up the notice.

I nod, and Jesse kneads his temples.

Mac grabs the paper. "Let me see that. Yanofsky? Oh shit, our moms are in book club together. My mom's gonna freak."

I cringe and lay my head on my knees.

Jesse pulls at his hair. "For those guys, it's their first time getting into trouble, so it's just a slap on the wrist. But me, I could get kicked out of school for, like, hate crimes. And your dad is friggin' going to hate me."

Justin, Mac and Tyler head down the hall, still swearing and jostling each other. Jesse watches me watch them. "Don't worry about them. They're just pissed off about getting caught." Jesse stands up. "Let's get out of here, go for a walk or something."

I stay sitting. "I don't feel so good. I think I'll hang out here."

Jesse nods and lopes down the hall after the guys. As soon as he's out of sight, I slip into the bathroom and dial Alexis. She picks up after the first ring.

"Hey Lauren, can I call you back? I'm—"

"No, this is an emergency."

"Okay, hold on a second." I hear her saying something, probably to Eric. "What's going on?"

"I did what you said, and now it's crazy. My father is coming to the school to talk about the Holocaust. My father!"

Alexis sighs. "Maybe they need to hear it."

"Are you nuts? No one needs more Holocaust."

"Take a few deep breaths and calm down."

"Lex, I'm beyond calming down. I've spent the last three years of my life trying to avoid the Holocaust, and now it's coming to my school. And it's my own fault!"

"It's not your fault those idiots pretended to be Nazis. Look, I think you're making way too big a deal about this. Kids will learn about hate crimes and then it will be over."

"It won't, and Jesse..."

"What about Jesse?"

"Forget it. I have to go now." I can't tell her the truth. It's too late, and I've told too many lies already.

When I get home, Zach is still in the garage. He's sleeping, so I leave a bag of chips and an apple beside his pillow. He hasn't eaten the sandwich I made him yesterday, but I guess he's been in the house eating whatever he likes. My parents aren't home yet, so I log on to Facebook. Alexis has posted a stupid picture of her cheer squad in uniform.

I scroll past Chloe's and Em's *Grease* comments, and then I see a post from Mike Choi: *I smell a rat.* Twenty-seven people "like" this, and there are an additional thirty-five comments, some from kids at school I don't know, kids who weren't at the park. Tyler comments, *People should keep their mouths shut.* Mac says, *Wonder who the bigmouth is?* I take a sharp breath in. What if someone says, *I bet it was Lauren?* I read more comments about *a rat* and *a fun game being ruined.* None of the comments are from Jesse. I check his status, but all it says is *grounded, again.*

Thirteen

The next morning I go straight to biology without going to my locker. Jesse is not in class because of his suspension, so I sit alone and work on an assignment.

In English class, Mr. Willoughby shows a film of *The Tempest*, but I can't concentrate. I haven't decided what I'm going to do this afternoon. Sit through my father's presentation? Get the hell out of here? I'm so anxious, I have a hard time sitting still. I excuse myself to go to the bathroom and choose the farthest one away so I can walk off some of my nervousness. It's not far enough; I have to get out of here now. I go back to class, gather up my bag and coat and explain to Mr. Willoughby that I feel sick.

"No vomiting in the room, thank you," he says and shoos me out. I trot down the closest stairs and burst out of the building. The cool air calms me a little, and I take a few massive breaths. It's a gray, damp day, the light flat, the mountains totally socked in.

I decide that if I stand under the trees at the edge of the field, I might feel better, might be able to make a clear decision about this afternoon, but as I start walking across the grass, I hear someone call my name.

I turn and see Brooke walking toward me, her bag in one hand, a cigarette in the other.

"Hey, where you going?"

"Oh, just away," I say.

"You're skipping?"

"Sort of." I start walking across the field.

Brooke jogs to catch up to me. "You never skip."

"Yeah, well, my dad's never been the guest lecturer at school either. Aren't you going?"

She shudders. "Nah, I can't sit through that."

"Why not?"

"I just can't."

"Oh."

"So where are you going?"

I shrug. "I don't know."

"We could go down to the beach..." Brooke looks thinner, as if she's been smoking instead of eating.

For a moment, I remember the way Brooke and I used to play together on the beach. A shot of pain passes through my head, making my temples ache. "Wouldn't you rather hang out with Kelly and Chantal?" I want to sound mean or sarcastic, but I can't keep the hurt out of my voice.

Brooke's expression doesn't change. She doesn't even wince. "They're in class," she says.

"Oh."

I look at Brooke carefully, and something about her unnerves me. It's not only the lack of response to my comment. It's also her heavy eye makeup, her black tights, her high boots. Her hair has lost its glossy shine. Mom would have a fit if she saw her.

Brooke seems to be waiting for me to say something else, so I say, "Fine, let's go." We walk silently to the corner and get on a bus heading toward the university. The trees along the streets are just naked branches against the gray sky. Brooke and I sit at the back of the almost-empty bus.

"So," I ask Brooke, "why can't you attend a Holocaust seminar?"

"I already know about that shit. I've seen the movies and everything." Brooke stares out the window.

"Oh."

"And my family."

"What about them?"

"Well, being German and all."

"I thought they were English."

"My dad's family is, but my mom's family is Polish and German."

"Oh."

"Yeah."

"Well, that doesn't matter to me."

"You're just saying that."

I scowl at her. "Hey, you weren't dressed up as a Nazi." I tug on the edge of her boots. "You've got your own new costume."

Brooke laughs. "Bet you're not so keen on that, either."

I shrug. "The eye makeup is brutal."

"At least you're honest."

I shrug. "I could be more honest."

"Yeah?" Brooke glances at me.

"I think you were a bitch about Jesse."

Brooke smacks a hand against her thigh. "You said you weren't interested!"

"Only because of the Nazi thing."

Brooke clenches her fists against her legs. "Well, it doesn't matter now. He certainly isn't interested in me."

"Yeah, I heard about that."

Brooke blushes. "Please don't remind me. It was *so* humiliating."

I hold on to that thought for a moment.

Brooke says, "It's good you guys are together. You know, being old friends and all. It makes a good story."

"Yeah, except for the Nazi part."

"I think you should let that go."

"I can't." I say this so fiercely, I surprise even myself.

Brooke squints at me, not understanding the determination in my voice. "The whole thing will blow over by next week."

"Hope so," I say. "Do you think you could arrange some other scandal to distract everyone?"

"Like what?"

"I don't know. Get caught smoking in the chem lab or make out with Kelly in the hall."

Brooke makes a face. "Gross!"

She stands up and moves toward the exit, motioning for me to follow her. We get off the bus at the edge of the campus by the water, a part I don't know well. Glimpses of the sea flash through the thick evergreen trees, like stars in a gray sky. Brooke pushes her hair out of her eyes and starts walking along the sidewalk. "I wonder who ratted the guys out."

I shrug, looking out at the sea.

"I heard someone turned in an armband with all the guys' names on it."

I swallow. "Pretty shitty."

"I keep wondering who would care enough to do that."

I turn to her and stop. "Well, maybe it was someone gay."

Brooke frowns. "What? Why would you say that?"

"Because the Nazis killed gay people too. Or maybe"—I arch my eyebrows—"it was someone Polish, because the Nazis killed lots of those too. No, I think it had to be someone disabled. Or a Communist, or an artist. Do you think any artistic people from our school were at the park that night?"

"I wasn't saying it was you."

I stare out at the sea. "I hate this whole crappy thing."

"I wasn't saying it was you."

"Yeah, whatever."

We stand on the sidewalk, cars zooming past us. Then Brooke says, "C'mon. Let's go down to the beach and stop talking about this." She points to a path a few meters ahead.

I follow Brooke to the path. "Is this the way to Wreck Beach?"

"Uh-huh."

"How do you know about it?"

"Sometimes Kelly and Chantal and I come down here to hang out."

The path through the trees is steep, and at the bottom there are some large boulders to climb over. Even though there isn't much wind, it's colder down here on the sand. Brooke and I perch on a damp log and listen to the hiss and pull of the waves slapping the shore, the seagulls screeching overhead. Brooke shivers in her thin jacket.

"Zach and I have been making lanterns," I tell her.

"Oh yeah, what kind?"

"Planes. Zach loves planes these days."

"Oh, that's cool."

"Actually, Zach has been making the lanterns. I suck at it."

Brooke nods. "You could take him to the festival next summer."

"Maybe," I say. "I'm not that into it anymore."

"How come?"

"I think I've had enough fire experiences." I hold up my bandaged hand.

"How did that happen?"

I consider telling Brooke about burning the book. "Just being careless."

"Oh."

The book reminds me of the armband and the fact that my father is talking about the Holocaust at my school—to Jesse and all the other kids—right now. What if Jesse's parents make him go back to boarding school? What if he finds out it was me who ratted him out?

"You know what I really want to burn?" I say.

"What's that?"

"I want to burn up the Holocaust."

"You mean at the lantern festival?"

"Yeah."

"How would you do that?"

"I don't know. Light a giant swastika on fire."

Brooke laughs and shakes back her hair. "I think people might try to kill you if you did that."

I nod. "And it wouldn't work anyway. Burning something doesn't make history or memory go away."

It starts to drizzle, so we head back up to the road and sit shivering in the bus shelter. The fog has lifted a little, and I can see down to the water.

Brooke and I both play with our phones on the bus ride home. I think about how Brooke and I will never go to the lantern festival again, or play on the beach. I can see it in her eyes. We're never going to go on an adventure together again.

When we get off the bus in front of Brooke's townhouse, I say, "You're still going to play basketball this year, right?" Cars are whipping past us, but I can only focus on Brooke.

"I think I might skip this year."

I rub my hands against my jeans. "That's crazy. You love basketball."

Brooke shakes her head. "You'll have fun without me."

I pull on my hair. "Why are you doing this?"

"Giving up basketball?"

"Well, everything. Giving up Chloe, Em, me." I feel like shaking Brooke, like waking her up from whatever alternate life she thinks she should live now.

"I told you, I'm not into praying and singing."

"Neither am I."

"I know, and I invited you to parties with Chantal and Kelly. I wanted you to come."

I nod slowly. "I guess you did." But that isn't the answer I'm looking for. "Thanks for the adventure then, and have a nice life."

"Hey, don't be like that."

"Yeah, okay." I try to smile, but it feels fake, like my face is just pretending when really I want to cry.

Brooke walks away and I sit down at the bus stop and put my head down on my knees for a moment. Sometimes the sadness I feel is so heavy, even though I know I'm a lucky person. I'm not feeling the anguish of being poor or hungry or sick, but still.

When I get home, Dad's car is in the driveway, and down the street I can see Jesse playing basketball. He waves and dribbles the ball toward me.

"Hey, where were you?" Jesse hugs the ball to his chest.

"I couldn't stay."

"Oh. Where did you go?"

"Just out with Brooke."

"With Brooke? I thought you guys weren't friends anymore."

"We're not."

Jesse gives me a funny look.

I ignore him. "How was the lecture?"

Jesse cocks his head to the side. "Well, parts of it were depressing—the movie and the history—but your dad's a good speaker. He was kinda uplifting at the end."

"Uplifting?"

"Yeah, he talked about fighting prejudice, that kind of stuff."

I nod. "Did everyone know he was my dad?"

"Yeah, I think so."

I cringe. "Great."

"I don't think that's what everyone's talking about right now."

"What are they talking about?"

"Oh, you know, who turned us in."

"Right. Yeah, I don't know. Are your parents still freaking out?"

"Nah, I think they're under control. I promised them extra-good behavior. I mean, I didn't fail any courses or steal anything. I'm grounded for two weeks, no parties or anything. But"—he smiles and hip-checks me—"they didn't say anything about you not coming over."

"Oh, good." I nod.

"So, what are you doing now?"

"Well, my dad's at home, and I think I should go talk to him, 'cause he'll know I wasn't at school."

"Maybe you could come over later, like after dinner."

"Maybe." I kick at the pavement. I know I don't sound very enthusiastic.

"Cheer up. I'm not going to boarding school, the lecture's over, so's my in-school suspension. It's all done."

"Great."

"What's with you?"

"Oh, just stuff with Brooke."

"Girls, man. You guys are rough on each other."

I nod. "See you later."

"Have fun with your dad." Jesse leans over to kiss me and I kiss him back, but I feel too guilty to enjoy it.

Dad is waiting for me in the front hall. He's wearing a shirt and tie, and his hair looks like he combed it. He says, "Hey," as I take off my jacket and boots.

"You're home early," I say.

"Well, I had this speaking engagement."

"Oh, where at?"

"Your school."

"Right." I nod. "I heard something about that." I start walking toward the kitchen. Dad follows me.

"While I was there, I looked for you. I'm pretty sure the letter said all grade eleven and twelve students were to attend."

I pour myself some water. "You're right, I wasn't there." I look at him squarely. "I missed Holocaust 101, right?"

Dad nods.

"Are you going to tell on me?"

He shakes his head, still smiling. "To whom?"

"I don't know."

Dad sits on a stool. "Did you know what was going on at school?"

"The seminar?"

"Lauren."

"Oh, you mean the armbands?"

"Yes, the armbands."

"I'm going to ask you a favor."

"Yes?"

"Please don't ask me that."

Dad sighs and loosens his tie. He points for me to sit next to him.

"Aren't we done yet?"

"No."

I reluctantly sit on the stool. Dad drums his fingers on the counter. "Here's what I'm thinking. One, you didn't know about the armbands, but I find that hard to believe. Two, you knew and you didn't do anything, and I find that harder to believe. Three, you knew and you did something about it, and I find that commendable and believable. And so, I'm going to say you did a good thing."

I stare into my water glass. "So there's no doubt now. Everyone at school knows about the Holocaust."

"The grade elevens and twelves anyway. Except for the ones who were skipping."

"Like Brooke."

"We'll invite her over for her own personal session."

"I don't think that's necessary. She's, like, a quarter German."

"And how does she feel about that?"

"Creepy."

"Is that one of the reasons you decided not to attend your own father's lecture?"

"One of them."

Dad sighs. "And do you think I came to school to make you feel uncomfortable and make Brooke feel guilty?"

"I kinda do. That might not have been your goal, but that's what happens. Now everyone knows they should treat Jews all special because people keep trying to wipe us out. It's like we've cornered the market on suffering."

Dad sighs again. "It's difficult to explain to you now what I was talking about at your school, since you decided not to attend, but if you had been there, you would have known I was there to promote tolerance, using the Holocaust as an example. One of my colleagues from the Holocaust center gives similar presentations about bullying."

"Well"—I sip my water—"Jesse did say the end of your talk was kinda uplifting."

"He wasn't skipping too?"

"No. He said you were a good speaker."

"He's a good kid. I think his boarding school helped straighten him out."

I look carefully at Dad's face to see if he knows Jesse was one of the kids playing the game. I don't think he does.

"If you're curious about the talk I gave, I'm giving it again at a school in Surrey next week."

"Oh, I'll think about it." I get up to leave, then sit back down. "Wait. There's something I don't get. If it's really about teaching tolerance, why can't you use some other tragedy as an example?"

"You could."

"But you don't."

"Well, I am a Holocaust historian. That's my field."

I nod. Fair enough. I start to stand up again, but Dad says, "I have a question for you."

"Yeah?"

"Why are you all of a sudden so squeamish about the topic?"

I knit my fingers together and squeeze. My hand still hurts, and I want to distract myself with pain. How to answer this without giving him a summary of how the Holocaust has affected me? I sigh. "I'm sick of the Holocaust being the defining element of being Jewish. It's like there's bagel and lox, and there's the Holocaust, and that's it."

Dad sighs. "You know, it doesn't have to be that way. There are lots of other parts to being Jewish."

"Like?"

"Well, for me, the most important part of being Jewish is social justice. I'm not really a spiritual person, but being ethical and helping others to be ethical is what makes me Jewish." Dad pauses a moment. "Maybe if you attended Jewish camp or youth group or Hebrew school, you wouldn't feel that the Holocaust was the only Jewish thing in your life."

I make a face. "I think I might convert to something else instead."

Dad rubs his forehead. "Please don't tell your mother that right now."

Both of us glance out at the garage. "Is Zach still out there?" I ask.

"I haven't checked yet."

"You want me to go out?"

"Not yet." Dad drums his fingers on the counter again. "You hungry?"

I shrug. "Sure."

Dad opens the freezer. "I don't think we have any lox, but we definitely have bagels."

Mom comes home a few minutes later and joins us at the counter. "How's your hand?" she asks me.

"Better."

"Good." She looks at Dad. "How was your lecture?"

"Fine, good."

She looks at me, and I nod. "Dad was great." Dad kicks me under the counter.

"Zach still out there?" She looks out the back window.

Dad says, "I haven't checked on him yet."

"Really? I came home early to see what was going on."

"Lauren and I were talking about other things. Besides, I'm pretty sure Zach's having a grand old time eating Cheezies and grapes." Dad holds up an empty grape bag.

"Actually, I ate those," I say.

"Oh."

Mom starts moving toward the back door. "Wait," I say. "Let me go out." Mom nods, and I head out to the garage. Zach's lying on an air mattress, in an old blue sleeping bag.

"Hey, I brought you an apple."

Zach lifts his head up. He looks pale and tired. "No, thanks."

I squat by his mattress. "You don't look good."

"It's the hunger strike."

"How long since you ate?"

"I scarfed a bag of chips Monday night."

"Nothing since then?"

"No, that wouldn't be fair."

"Zach, that was days ago, so you're kidding, right?"

Zach closes his eyes and shakes his head.

"I told you to cheat!" I punch the air mattress by his head.

Zach rolls over on his side. "It has to be real, so they'll see I'm serious. And I've been drinking a lot, so I'm not dehydrated. According to my research, I should be okay for another two weeks."

Zach's surrounded himself with comic books and water bottles, but he looks too listless to move. I want to shake him, but I know that won't work. Instead I say, "Can I talk to you for a bit?" Zach nods, and I sit next to him. The garage is damp, and I shiver. "How long are you going to go on?"

"Until they give in."

"No bar mitzvah?"

"No monkey show."

"It's the people, right?"

Zach nods.

I tap my fingers on my knees. "What if there weren't a lot of people? Would you do it then?"

"What do you mean?"

"Say there were only a few guests."

"I guess that wouldn't be so bad."

I rub my fingernails against each other. "So it's not the learning you're against."

Zach shrugs.

"I think I may have a plan. I'll be right back." I race into the house and get my Tanach—my Hebrew Bible—and crouch down next to Zach. "Okay, what if we open this at random? Could you read it?"

"Can I go over it once?"

"Sure."

Zach rolls over on his stomach and props himself up on his elbows. I watch as he reads through the Hebrew. Even though I attended Hebrew school for eight years, I still had to study hard to learn how to chant the Hebrew. I watch Zach's lips moving.

"Okay, I think I can do the first part," he says.

"Go for it." I follow along in the text as Zach chants half a page effortlessly, using the correct musical notation. "Wow."

Zach lies back down and closes his eyes. "It's not hard."

"Could you do it without the notes?" When you read from a Torah scroll, there's no musical notation for the chanting. You just have to know it.

"I already memorized it."

"Right." I pause for a moment.

"What are you thinking?" Zach asks.

"Mom and Dad want you to have a bar mitzvah. And you don't mind doing the reading, but you don't want it to be a gong show, right?"

"Right."

"Okay, so you could learn this fast and have your bar mitzvah soon to get it over and done with, right?"

"Yeah…"

"So then the next question is, how many guests do you think you could handle?"

Zach thinks for a second. "Seventeen."

"Seventeen?"

"Yep."

"That's the exact number?"

"Yep. Any more and I can't do it."

"Can you tell me why?"

"When I had to do a speech for the speech contest, there were seventeen kids in the class, and that was fine."

"Okay. Gotcha. What about the party?"

"No party."

"Mom won't buy that."

Zach hangs his head.

"Wait. What if the party was here, and you had to say hi to people, but then when you'd had enough, you could go to your room or come out here?"

Zach presses his lips together. "That might be okay. If there were only seventeen people."

"Do you think you could handle twenty?"

"Maybe. But only if I get to choose. And I don't have to wear a suit."

"Zach, you can wear a suit. And have your picture taken. And lead the whole service."

Zach closes his eyes. For a moment I think he might be falling asleep or passing out. Then he looks at me and grimaces. "I guess I could."

"Deal?"

"Deal." Zach sticks out a weak hand and we shake.

In the kitchen, Mom is making pasta while Dad grates cheese.

Mom says, "Is he coming in yet?"

I sit on a stool at the counter. "Not yet. Here's the situation. Zach hasn't eaten in over forty-eight hours. For real."

Mom puts down her knife. "Oh my god."

"He's been drinking water, so I think he'll be okay, but we need to step up negotiations."

Mom turns to Dad. "*Leave him and he'll be fine.* Isn't that what you said?"

Dad throws up his hands. "How was I supposed to know he wasn't eating?"

"Hello?" I wave my hands between them. "I think I have a solution." I wait until they both turn to me. "Zach says he'll have a bar mitzvah, but it has to be small and soon."

Mom frowns. "How small?"

"Seventeen people. He's agreed to a party, but it has to be here. Also, he says he'll wear a suit, pose for photos and lead the whole service."

Dad whistles. "Maybe you should go into labor negotiations."

"I'd be good."

"You'd be excellent."

I can see Mom calculating which seventeen family and friends to invite. She sighs. "Well, I guess that would be fine. It's the ceremony that's important. Did he really say seventeen people?"

"I think he might be persuaded to twenty. But it has to be soon."

"Why's that?" Dad asks.

"So he can get it over with. I think the anticipation's killing him."

Mom flails her arms in the air. "But he hasn't even started studying. And you need time to plan these things."

"Not if you only have seventeen people. You've had dinner parties bigger than that. And don't worry about the studying. Zach has already taught himself how to read the Torah."

"Oh?"

"Yep."

"Well," Dad says, "that would be Zach." He turns to Mom. "Deal?"

She braces her hands on the counter and closes her eyes for a minute. "What about a speech?"

"I wouldn't push it," I say.

Mom pauses, then sighs. "Fine. I guess that'll have to be good enough."

Dad says, "Let's feed him and get him back in here then."

I quickly make Zach a peanut-butter-and-banana sandwich, his favourite, and he eats it out in the garage, along with three chocolate-chip cookies and a glass of milk. When he feels a little better, I help him carry his sleeping bag and comics back into the house.

After dinner I log on to Facebook. I'm expecting more Holocaust-related comments, but Mac's posted a stupid cartoon and Tyler's written about a hockey game. Chloe's status says she's off to a youth-group sleepover this weekend. Brooke and Chantal are talking about a party in Ladner. I scroll all the way down and find Tyler's *I smell a rat* comment from yesterday. There are fifty-seven posts now. I crinkle up my toes and look around me. Zach has gone to bed, Dad's in his office, and Mom's on the phone in the kitchen, madly rebooking Zach's bar mitzvah. I skip the posts I read yesterday and look at the new ones. Chloe wrote, *Bad idea to start with*. Brooke added, *Superbad taste*. Even Chantal and Kelly weighed in. *Serves you right, losers*, Kelly said. Chantal wrote, *Get a life*. A girl named Cass from my English class wrote, *It wasn't a rat, it was someone who decided not to be a bystander*. I click *Like* under Cass's comment. Then I update my status. *I'm thinking about a career in labor relations.*

The chat box comes up from Alexis. *How was your dad's talk?*

Didn't go.

U skipped?

Yep.

Wow. Where did u go? Alexis has probably never skipped in her life.

To the beach with Brooke. Then I tell her about Zach's hunger strike and his bar mitzvah, which is going to be in two weeks. Alexis writes, *Glad things worked out ok*, and since I can't think of anything to else to say, I write back, *Yep.*

I go into the kitchen to get a snack and see how Mom's doing. She's sitting at the counter with the phone and her bar mitzvah planning notebook beside her. I can tell from her red eyes that she's been crying. Also, her hair is scrunched up on one side from resting her head in her hand.

"How goes it?"

Mom sighs. "I cancelled the country club, most of the catering order, the invitations and napkins. I called the rabbi, and luckily no one wanted a date in November. We're going to have the service in the downstairs chapel, not the main sanctuary."

I nod my head. "Sounds good."

Mom continues. "I called Auntie Susan and Uncle Steve and Dan and Cathy, and they're going to come."

I nod again.

"I lost the deposit for the country club, but I guess that doesn't matter."

"You could have a party for something else there. Maybe your anniversary or Dad's birthday or something."

Mom stops tucking papers into her notebook. "You don't get it, do you?"

"Get what?" I stop eating my cereal.

Mom squints at me over her reading glasses. "Look, you may not know this, but life can be pretty shitty." I put down my spoon. Mom almost never swears. She continues, hands braced on the counter. "Most people in the world are poor or sick or live in countries at war. People die all the time. And my job is to try and convince girls not to starve themselves to death. I counsel them and teach them about good nutrition. And some of the time, the girls get better. And other times, the girls kill themselves. Lots of life is like that: miserable."

I'm not sure where Mom is going with this. I've never heard her talk so bitterly. She continues. "And then there are some amazing times in life, like when a baby is born or people get married. Those times should be celebrated, and because we're Jewish, we also celebrate our children with a bar or bat mitzvah."

"Because we're adults now?"

Mom ignores my snarky tone. "You know, I don't think it's about becoming an adult. I think it's the parents' way of celebrating the success of childhood. Your kid didn't die of some horrible disease and learned how to read and write and, if they were lucky, how to ride a bike and swim. By twelve or thirteen, kids need to start being independent. And that's it; a parent's most important role is over. If you haven't done your job up to that point, well, you've missed your opportunity. And this—this growing up should be celebrated. All that other crappy stuff about life—the dying and sickness—for one day you get to ignore it and celebrate your child. And that's why I wanted to have a big bar mitzvah for Zach. To celebrate everything he's done, because it's been harder for him than most kids." Mom's voice starts to crack. "That's all I wanted."

I want to tell her that Zach's bar mitzvah will still be a celebration, just smaller, but I can see she feels cheated out of her months of planning. All of her excitement and enthusiasm has been squelched to a measly few weeks and seventeen guests in the dinky chapel. "I think the party here will be nice."

Mom looks up from shuffling her papers. "I'm sure it will be." She picks up her notebook. "I'm going to bed. Don't stay up too late."

I nod and think about everything Mom has said, about making a party for Zach. It's true Zach needs to be celebrated, just in a special way. I tap my fingers on the counter and think about the lantern planes Zach has been making, about how to make them part of the celebration for Zach, who dreams of flying.

Fourteen

On Saturday, Jesse asks me to go running in Pacific Spirit Park, a forest with trails near the university. As I pull on my running tights, I smile and think, This is so normal—me going for a run with my boyfriend.

Jesse honks in front of the house, and I slide into the front seat of his mom's van. It's another gray day, the overcast sky threatening rain. Jesse squeezes my knee when I get in and then focuses on the road. He seems quieter than usual, less excited to see me, and I clench my hands into fists at my sides.

We drive in silence, and I wish I could think of something cheerful to say. Finally, Jesse asks, "So, Zach still on his hunger strike?"

"No, he finished Thursday night."

"What was that about?"

"Oh, he didn't want to have a bar mitzvah."

"So is it cancelled?"

"Nah, just smaller—and sooner." I start to relax, letting my fists unfurl.

Jesse nods. "I remember your bat mitzvah."

"You do?"

"Sure. My whole family was invited."

"What did you think of it all?"

"I remember thinking that your parents must really love you to shower all that attention on you."

I glance at Jesse, feeling myself redden. "I always felt it was more about showing off. 'Look what my kid can do.'"

"I didn't think that. Your parents looked so proud of you. Mine were too busy fighting to even notice me."

"Oh."

"Yeah, well, unless I got into trouble. Then I got a lot of attention..." He sighs.

I raise my eyebrows.

Jesse says, "It's nothing. Just bad memories." But he is still somber.

I'm not sure what to say, so we drive the rest of the way in silence. When we get to the park, we get out of the car and stretch our legs at the edge of the forest. Even with mitts and toques on, we're chilled in our light jackets, so when Jesse raises his eyebrows to ask if I'm ready, I nod. We start down the dirt path, my legs stiff and reluctant to move. I force myself forward, knowing I'll loosen up in a few minutes. The ground is hard from the cold but easier on the joints than running on pavement is, like I usually do. We don't talk; there's just our breath puffing out warm clouds into the damp November air. The moss hanging from the tree branches makes the forest feel like an underwater cave, like we're pushing through curtains of seaweed.

The path opens up to a wider gravel road, and the air around us seems to lighten without the gloom of the trees. Jesse and I pick up the pace. My limbs are loose and warm now, and a light sweat breaks out along my back. I start to relax. We pass a few dog walkers and some parents with kids in strollers.

In the end, we run farther than planned because the route Jesse mapped out finishes on the other side of the park. I groan when we realize his mistake.

"What, can't take it, Yanofsky?" Jesse says, and he sprints down the path.

"Hey, wait up!" I dart through the trees, trying to keep him in view. He slows down so I can catch up. We're too tired for wind sprints, so we jog for a while and then walk back to the car.

I grab Jesse's hand and smile at him. "That was a good run."

Jesse nods. "We're going to be so fast on the court."

"Either that or ready for track season."

"You do track?"

"I didn't last year, but I might this year. You know"—
I think about Chloe and Em's youth-group schedule—
"keep busy."

Jesse nods. I can tell he's brooding about something,
and I feel my stomach twist. Finally he stops on the trail
and turns to me. "You know how I had to go to boarding
school because I failed a bunch of classes?"

"Yeah." I clasp my hands behind my back.

"I wasn't only in trouble for that. That was just the
last thing."

"Oh." Jesse seems to be waiting for me to say something else, so I ask, "What else did you do?"

Jesse grins nervously. "I stole some stuff, just stupid
things, to see if I could get away with it."

"What did you steal?"

"Eyedrops from the nurse's office, a school microscope and Mr. Yip's cell phone."

I can't help smiling. Mr. Yip was the guidance coun-
selor when we were in grade nine. "Why did you do that?"

"I don't know. Bored, mostly. Curious, you know, to
see what would happen."

I nod and start walking, but Jesse grabs my hand.
"Don't you want to know why I'm telling you this?" His
cheeks are red from the cold air; he's not smiling.

I flex my legs nervously. "I don't know. I thought you
were just telling me stuff."

Jesse drops my hand and starts walking away. Then he turns back. "I want to ask you something, and I think I already know the answer. And I don't want you to be mad, so I thought maybe I should tell you something about me—something kinda crappy."

I tense my shoulders. "You think you know something crappy about me?"

"I think I do."

I stay silent for an incredibly long time. The wind rustles the trees and I shiver, my sweat turning cold on my back. Could someone please tell me the right answer? No, this is a lose-lose situation. Confess, and I'm a traitor. Say nothing, and things only get worse. Finally I say, "I burned my hand setting fire to one of my father's books."

Jesse's face softens. "That's so not what I thought you were going to say. You burned a book?"

I nod.

"Wow, why did you do that?"

I take a deep breath. "I didn't like what was inside it. Holocaust crap. And I thought if I burned the book, maybe I'd stop thinking about it."

"Did it work?"

"No."

Jesse digs his running shoe into the gravel. "Lauren, that isn't what I was going to ask you."

I'm so nervous, I can't say a word. I squeeze my hands so tightly that I accidentally crack one of my knuckles.

Jesse takes a deep breath. "You turned in the armband, didn't you?"

I freeze, looking up at him.

"Look, I don't know if it was you, and maybe it's a shitty thing to ask, but I can't think of anyone else who would have done it."

I look up at the towering trees, tilting my head back until I feel dizzy. If I was a stronger person, I'd say, *Yeah, I did* and look back at him defiantly. But I'm not like that, and tears well in my eyes. I'm standing on the path, crying into my mittens, and I'm sure Jesse is thinking, Jeez, can't we even talk about this? Or, Why do girls always start to cry?

I gulp, trying to swallow back my tears, searching for the right words. Eventually Jesse says, "C'mon. I'm starting to freeze."

We jog back to the road, my face still wet from crying, and get in the car without stretching our legs. I feel my muscles bunch and tighten as I sit shivering.

Jesse turns the car on, but I put my hand over his. "Wait."

"You don't have to say anything," he mumbles.

"Yes, I do."

Jesse turns off the motor, and I sigh and wipe my cheeks with my mittens. "When I was twelve," I start quietly, "my dad took me to this Holocaust memorial with my grandmother." I tell him about Grandma Rose crying on the stone, about how obsessed I became, how I read everything about the Holocaust, how anxious it made me. I leave out the part about the panic attacks. Jesse faces forward, listening but not looking at me. Outside, rain starts to fall. "I didn't know what to say about the game, that first time in the park. I didn't think you were really being Nazis, but it was still too much. And yeah, you apologized, but it seemed so halfhearted. That's why I told Brooke I wasn't interested in you. How could I be with a guy who thought pretending to be a Nazi wasn't a big deal?"

"Is that why Brooke was coming on to me? She thought you didn't like me anymore?"

"Well, yeah. But then we went for that run down at the beach before the party. I was so confused when you left the party with Brooke."

"And that's when you decided to turn in the armband?"

I nod. "I felt so…disposable."

"Disposable?"

"Like so many girls were in love with you, you could kiss me and then hook up with someone else and not care."

Jesse presses his lips together. "Had you ever seen me do that?"

"No."

"But you thought I was like that anyway?" His lip curls up.

I pull my knees up to my chin and drop my head down. "I guess so."

Jesse sighs, then slouches in his seat. "Is that it?"

"Yes, that's it." I hesitate. "Are we done talking about this?"

"Yep, we're done." There's a grimness around Jesse's mouth, and I'm not sure how to read it. Does it mean we're done talking about this, or that we're done for good?

Jesse starts the car and pulls into the traffic. He keeps his eyes on the road the whole way home, and I focus on trying not to cry. When we get to my house, I get out of the car without even looking at him. Then I slink up the stairs, lock myself in the bathroom and get in the shower. As soon as the hot water starts to pound down, I let myself cry, sobbing as if the world is ending.

I spend the rest of the weekend crying in my room, alternating between hoping Jesse will text or call and trying to convince myself that he never will. He doesn't. I call Alexis and tell her everything. When she says I did the right thing, I hang up on her in a burst of fresh tears. When I'm not crying, I stress about sitting next to Jesse in biology and whether he'll tell the other guys I turned in the armband. I check Facebook over and over, but no one has any new comments about the armbands.

On Sunday evening Zach comes into my room, carrying the wooden frame of a star lantern. "I made your lantern for you," he says. "I thought we could do the tissue part together." I look up from my damp pillow. Zach's made the frame of a star lantern, but it's a six-sided Jewish star, not the five-sided star I'd imagined.

I start to cry again. "It's not supposed to be a Jewish star, it's supposed to be a regular star, five-sided," I whimper.

"Oh." Zach lifts up the lantern and peers into it. "I couldn't find your design. No wonder all the measurements were funny." He hesitates. "I could fix it maybe or make another one."

"Don't bother," I grumble.

Zach's face falls. "I just wanted to cheer you up, so you'd stop crying," he says.

"I'm not crying," I mutter into my pillow.

"Yes you are."

"Zach, go away."

He leaves quietly, and I feel even worse for being mean to him.

By Monday morning I'm exhausted from crying. My eyes ache, and my face feels as stiff as a mask. I get ready for school, going through the motions of eating and dressing. At school I go straight to the biology lab and sit on my stool with my coat on. Jesse comes and sits down next to me but doesn't glance my way. I feel like crying again, but I'm too tired. Instead I focus on breathing calmly, until Mr. Saunders announces we'll start the fetal pig dissection tomorrow. Then I let my head fall to the lab table. I can't work with Jesse, but I also can't dissect a disgusting dead pig myself. I'm feeling desperate enough to ask Brooke and Chantal if I can work with them, but they're not here today.

At lunchtime I don't bother going back to my locker. I just walk out of English class and head home. I eat my lunch in front of the TV, staring blankly at a talk show.

Two weeks pass in the same suspended state: school, lunch at home, running and homework after school. My hand heals enough for me to start playing basketball, and I shoot hoops alone in my driveway for hours. Chloe and Em press for details about why Jesse and I aren't talking; I tell them we had a fight. Jesse and I do the dissection together without making eye contact. Actually, Jesse does the dissection and I watch, a hand over my mouth. When an involuntary "Ew" escapes me at the first incision, he stops to glare at me. He hates me, I think, and I can't blame him. He cuts up the rest of the pig according to the handout and points things out in a monotone, without looking at me. After a while he becomes so engrossed, I think he forgets I'm there. He even asks Mr. Saunders if he can take his pig home to get help from his dad, who is a doctor. Mr. Saunders says, "No, dissections can't leave the school or even the room. Remember grade eight? Remember the cow's eyeballs in the cafeteria?"

Jesse blushes and says, "Gotcha."

The only good news is that Brooke has hooked up with this guy Ray, so everyone's talking about them and not the Nazi armbands. Ray's new at our school, and according to rumors, he's nineteen and does hard drugs. Brooke skips the entire week of biology and pig dissection. Chloe says she's heard Brooke's living with her dad, which is crazy because she hates him. It's as if Brooke's a different person now, one I don't know anymore.

At home, everyone focuses on Zach's bar mitzvah preparations. Zach works every afternoon with his tutor on his Torah portion and the prayers, although he refuses to meet Rabbi Birenbaum. Eventually Zach compromises (with my help) and chants his Torah portion for the rabbi over Skype. Mom and Dad have their fingers crossed that Zach will shake hands with Rabbi Birenbaum, but I think it's unlikely. The guest list swells to twenty-four, but Zach doesn't seem to mind. The only people he wants to invite are his teachers from school.

Mom plans an airplane-themed party with vintage-aircraft napkins and a giant biplane cake. She even finds a biplane tie Zach likes. Dad books a jazz trio to play in the front hall for the party, and I work on the decorations with Mom, which is a good distraction. Mom loves my suggestion of hanging Zach's plane lanterns in the backyard. It's too cold to have the party outside, but the lanterns will glow through the glass at the back of the house and look really cool. I also suggest we line the front walk with paper-bag lanterns, like at the lantern festival. We sit up late one night eating popcorn and using a hole punch to cut Stars of David and airplanes into the bags. I cut a few bags with the five-pointed stars I originally designed for a lantern. Mom tries to ask me about Jesse, but I hold up my hand. "I don't want to talk about it." She doesn't press any further.

When we're finished all the bags, we go outside to the front steps and light a candle in one of the bags to try it out. Goose bumps run up my arms as a golden biplane glows through the lantern. I want to light all the bags right then in a circle on the front lawn and lie down in the middle of them.

The Friday before Zach's bar mitzvah, Mom and I have appointments with the hairdresser; then we all have family photos—Zach's promised not to tell me to fuck off—and finally a family dinner at Aunt Susan and Uncle Steve's house. Zach is excited and formally greets each of our aunts and uncles at the dinner, shaking their hands. He's wearing his biplane tie, even though it's supposed to be for tomorrow, because he likes it so much. "Tomorrow is my bar mitzvah," he tells everyone, as if they didn't already know. Zach looks so happy that for the first time since the run with Jesse, I feel my spirits lift.

Back at home, Zach retreats to his video games and Mom and Dad drink scotch in the living room with my Aunt Barb and Uncle Dan, who are staying with us. I get into my pajamas and read in my room for a while, but I'm too excited to sleep, so I wander down to the basement and sit at the workbench. Next to Zach's plane lanterns lies the frame of the star lantern he made for me. He's glued it together so neatly, even building in a space for a candle. I sigh and decide to finish it up, to say thank you to Zach. I work until past midnight, carefully gluing on blue tissue in neat strips and adding a string to hang it. When I'm done, I leave it outside Zach's door so he'll see it in the morning.

Saturday morning Zach leads the whole service and chants his Torah portion without once looking up at the congregation. When he finishes chanting, Mom has to call his name so that he'll look up and see us throwing candies at him. I manage to hit him right in the head with a Lieber's gummy candy, his favourite. Then we all have to wait while Zach chews the candy he's stuffed in his mouth. Zach does manage to shake the rabbi's hand, but he decides to skip the second half of the lunch and walk all the way home. We find him sleeping in a lawn chair in the backyard when we get home an hour later.

By 7:00 PM our house is a flurry of party preparations. The jazz trio is hanging out in the living room, and the caterers have taken over the kitchen and dining room, setting out trays for the party that has swelled to thirty guests. Zach doesn't care about the party because Dad has given him an incredibly complicated new model-plane kit and set him up at a card table in a corner of the dining room. At first Mom doesn't like the way the card table and the messy kit look, but Dad explains, "This way he'll stay downstairs for most of the night, or at least until he finishes the kit."

Mom beams. "Brilliant!" Then they kiss even though the caterers can see them from the kitchen.

Once I'm dressed in the beautiful black velvet cocktail dress with spaghetti straps that Mom bought me, I head to the front yard to set out the paper-bag lanterns and hang Zach's star. The planes are already hanging in the backyard.

It's a beautiful night, crisp and clear, with the stars glimmering through the bare tree branches. I shiver as the night air cools my bare arms.

Just as I'm hanging the star lantern from a branch of the Japanese maple beside our front door, I hear someone on the path behind me. I imagine it's an early guest, but when I turn around, Jesse is standing on the flagstones.

I draw in my breath. "You scared me."

"Oh, sorry. Hey, you look really nice."

"Thanks. It's Zach's bar mitzvah party tonight." Jesse also looks great. He's wearing the toque that makes his hair fall into his eyes the way I like. I start to blush, so I turn away from him and focus on lighting the candle in the star lantern. The candle glows and flickers, making the tree's shadows look ghostly beautiful.

"Did you make that?" Jesse points to the star.

"Well, sort of. I started it—it was supposed to be a five-pointed star—but Zach finished it, and, well, it turned into a Jewish star instead."

"It looks cool."

"Thanks."

"So," Jesse says slowly, "what are you doing now?"

"Well, I have to finish up some decorations. People will be here soon."

"Oh, I should go then." Jesse starts backing away.

"You could help me, if you wanted to," I blurt out.

"Um, sure."

I hand Jesse a stack of the paper-bag lanterns. "We need to set these up along the walkway and then light candles inside them." I show him how to fold the tops of the bags out to keep them open. Jesse nods and takes the bags, and we work silently in the dim light, adding the candles and then lighting them with Dad's long barbecue lighter. I don't look at Jesse the whole time, because I need to keep my nervousness under control. When all the lanterns are lit, I step onto the sidewalk. Jesse follows me and we stand in silence, gazing up the walkway. The lanterns glow like a row of little bonfires, leading up to the star in the tree. The effect is enchanting, and I shiver and wrap my arms tight around myself.

Jesse asks quietly, "Why a star lantern?"

At first I can't think of an answer. I shrug. I mull it over, trying not to think about why Jesse is here, although I can feel a flicker of excitement start to burn in my heart. I look up at him. "Maybe because it's something that burns, but it's beautiful and far away and doesn't hurt anyone."

Jesse nods. "I tried texting you before I came over, but I didn't hear back from you."

"My phone's up in my room." I hesitate. "Why did you text?"

"I wanted to know if I could come over."

"Oh. So here you are."

"Yeah." Jesse pauses. "I guess I just wanted to see you."

I smile and hold out my arms. "Well, here I am." I spin around on one of my high heels. Jesse smiles at me, and then he reaches out one hand and pulls me toward him. He wraps his arms around me, pressing me to him. It's more of a big squeeze than a hug, almost too rough, but it says everything I want it to, and that's enough for now. We stand there, locked in each other's arms, for what feels like forever. When he finally lets me go, I silently take his hand and lead him back to the front yard, into the midst of the flickering lanterns. We stand there, not looking at each other, not speaking, just admiring the glow of the small flames.

Acknowledgments

Many thanks to Carole Lieberman, Lucien Lieberman, Dianne Scott, Sarah Tsiang and Jeff Waller for their advice and suggestions on this book. I am especially grateful to Sarah Harvey for her careful editing and to Pamela Paul for her support.

Leanne Lieberman is the author of two other novels for young adults, *Gravity* and *The Book of Trees*. She lives in Kingston, Ontario, with her husband and two sons. For more information, visit www.leannelieberman.com.